MW01452032

ADVENTURES WITH BOYS # 3

ADVENTURES WITH BOYS # 3

Microworlds Atom-Force

G. L. Strytler

Copyright © 2007 by G. L. Strytler.

ISBN: Hardcover   978-1-4257-5646-8
         Softcover   978-1-4257-5644-4

All rights reserved. No part of this book may be reproduced or transmitted in any form or by any means, electronic or mechanical, including photocopying, recording, or by any information storage and retrieval system, without permission in writing from the copyright owner.

This is a work of fiction. Names, characters, places and incidents either are the product of the author's imagination or are used fictitiously, and any resemblance to any actual persons, living or dead, events, or locales is entirely coincidental.

This book was printed in the United States of America.

To order additional copies of this book, contact:
Xlibris Corporation
1-888-795-4274
www.Xlibris.com
Orders@Xlibris.com
39286

CONTENTS

1   Auratoss 7
2   Jaunt 17
3   The Battle of Rolin 22
4   The New Recruits 29
5   Deltena 36
6   Communication 44
7   Diabolic 53
8   The Albeta Warfare Evasion 58
9   The Moon Probe 68
10 Anti-Orbit Gears..76
11 Galla 82
12 Marrek's Mercantile 90
13 The Land of Suca 97
14 Suca's Trunk 104
15 The Land of Puppets..111
16 Stormfront...119
17 Nocturnal Riots 126
18 Atom 135
19 The Final Game..140
20 Stasia..149

1

Auratoss

The dark, deep-set, brown house slowly grew lighter and lighter as the sun erased all the shadows of the night. Devon Steinbrook walked up the path to the front door, reached in his pocket and pulled out a piece of paper, unfolded it, and struggled to read the writing on the note in the early morning light.

478 Wedgewood Lane; this was the right address. He knocked on the door and waited a few minutes before the door flew open.

"Good Morning, sir, I hope I didn't wake you," Devon said politely.

"No, not at all," the man at the door replied. "I've been expecting you. Come in, please."

Devon entered the large house and removed his hat to reveal his light brown hair. From the outside, the house looked as though it had many rooms, but from the inside, it appeared altogether different. Gold trim made the large white room that much more elaborate. Devon noticed the windows high in the ceiling. They had been the windows he had seen from the outside, giving the house the effect of more rooms.

The owner of the home, and obvious scientist, stood about six feet tall with somewhat shaggy salt and pepper black hair, green eyes, and very stylistic glasses that he mostly used for reading.

Devon walked directly to the living room and sat down on the large brown sofa. Setting his briefcase on the coffee table, he took out a small stack of papers and leaned back on the soft brown exterior.

"Mr. Braddock McGee," Devon said, clearing his throat. "I've been receiving a lot of letters from you for awhile about this special project you've been working on. You told me in these letters that the project was to enhance pictures, is that true?"

"Well, yes," Braddock answered. "The project I've been working on can develop pictures that in no other way can be developed properly because the negatives turned out blurry or became warped due to heat. To simplify, it can clarify damaged photos in general."

"Negatives or not?" Devon said.

"Right," Braddock said, folding his arms.

"Yes, that's what I thought," Devon stated, rearranging his stack of papers. "As you know, I work for E.R.T. and Associates. Our firm specializes in bringing new products to market, especially in the area of bringing criminals to justice. I don't know how we could use this project right now, but I would still like to give it a trial run."

Devon handed Braddock a black and white photo that had made its way to the top of the stack of papers Devon had been holding.

"This is a picture of a man who is responsible for a number of bank robberies. This is the only known photo of him. And since he hasn't robbed a bank in a little over a year, the courts want to throw the case out. When I received your letters, our firm decided to give it one last chance." Devon paused and looked at Braddock. "So, what do you think?" Braddock smiled a crooked smile with a sign of great pride in his eyes.

"So, if I can get a decent picture out of this, your agency will help bring my project to market?"

"I make no guarantees, but I'll see what I can do," Devon said, placing his papers back into his briefcase. "It will take some time, I assure you, but there's been a great deal of money lost on this jerk and I want to find him if he hasn't already left the country."

Braddock glanced across the room, opposite of where Devon had come in. "Follow me," he stated in a low, rough voice.

Devon stood, leaving a dent in the cushion, and followed Braddock across the room into a garage that had been turned into a small shop.

"This is it! This is the machine I've been working on for the last two years."

Devon looked at the machine on the far wall. It stood close to nine feet high and about fifteen feet across. "It's a lot bigger that I had imagined," he said.

"That's because it can do a lot of other things. I'll tell you about those later, but first I want to show you something." Braddock opened a drawer in a nearby shelf and pulled out what looked like a small lens. He then attached it to part of the machine.

Devon examined the machine closely as Braddock tightened a small bolt. He noticed all the small parts and details that had gone into the making.

He also noticed the whole machine looked somewhat old-fashioned and homemade.

"This took two years to build?" Devon asked, turning his attention once again to Braddock.

"Yes," Braddock said, finishing his task and turning to Devon. "Days and Nights, but I think it was all worth it. It was an idea I had come up with three years ago, just to create a mega-machine that can do small odd jobs. But as time went on, plans changed, and it didn't turn out the way I expected it to. Now I just use different parts of the machine for different things," Braddock said, stepping back. "There it is!" he said, glorifying his work with odd hand gestures. "Now, let me give you a demonstration." He turned and walked back across the room and picked up a large piece of paper that had half of a dark green fingerprint on it. He laid the paper carefully under the lens. "I had my fingerprint enlarged on this paper specifically for such a demonstration. The machine will guess at the other half. Let me fingerprint myself so we can compare the end result." Braddock placed his right thumb on the pad of cold green ink and stamped it onto a smaller piece of paper.

The machine began to quietly hum as a small red laser beam moved smoothly over the paper, etching a charcoal brown print on the other half. Nobody uttered a word until the machine came to a silent stop.

Braddock removed the warm paper from below the lens and proudly handed it to Devon.

Devon walked over to the table, picked up a magnifying glass and began to closely examine every detail as Braddock nervously paced back and forth.

"It's no good!" Devon said, breaking the silence.

"What? What do you mean 'it's no good'?" Braddock demanded. "I didn't spend two years of my life building and researching to find out my project is no good!"

Devon laid the magnifying glass back on the table. "I'm sorry, the two sides of the print don't match your fingerprints at all."

Braddock grabbed the magnifying glass and studied the fingerprint closely, then picked up the copy and examined every detail. *"Devon was right!"* Braddock thought. *"Nothing about these two were the same."*

"What do you say we try your machine on the picture I brought." Devon said.

Braddock looked up at Devon. "You really want to try, especially after the monstrosity you've just seen?"

"I've got nothing else to go on. I've got to at least try, and this is my last chance," Devon said, as he watched Braddock smile. "I left the picture in my briefcase," he continued.

Braddock smiled once more and led Devon back to the living room and over to the coffee table . . . Braddock suddenly froze. A very strange feeling overcame him. It wasn't bad and it wasn't quite good. He could feel it creeping over his body from his toes to the tip of his head, sending spine-tingling ripples through every nerve in his entire body. It was a sensation Braddock had never felt before. He turned and looked at Devon in the eyes and could tell he sensed it as well.

A deafening explosion suddenly echoed through the house with a blinding flash of light, sending Devon flying head over heels backwards.

When the explosion finally subsided, Braddock awoke looking up into a thick black smoke. He laid there silently, watching the cloud roll around until it slowly disappeared. He tried to stand up, grasping the counter for support, and found himself in the kitchen just off the living room. He focused his eyes and glanced around the house until he noticed Devon lying next to the sofa.

"Are you alright!" he shouted.

"Yeah . . . I'm fine, I just took a nasty blow to the head from something, probably from my briefcase," Devon said with a chuckle.

They both stood to observe the damage and gasped to find nothing had been moved or damaged. The force that had thrown the two men across the room had not moved lamps or dropped picture frames that were still hanging perfectly straight on the walls. The plaster from the walls didn't even show signs of the smallest crack or burn, which was odd after an explosion of that magnitude.

Braddock turned back to Devon and noticed the side of his head had been cut and was bleeding. "You did take a nasty blow to the head," he said, examining the wound. "I've got some bandages in my first aid kit."

Devon followed Braddock to the kitchen and watched as he took the blue box from the bottom drawer. "I'm terribly sorry about this inconvenience," Devon shyly stated.

"I'm sorry too, but it's no inconvenience," Braddock responded. Braddock looked back around the room one more time as he finished bandaging Devon's head. "Finished!" he said after a few minutes. "How does that feel?"

"It stings a bit, but it's fine."

"Well, let's check out the shop. I believe that's where the explosion came from."

The two men entered the doorway and beheld the same sight they had seen in the living room and kitchen. Nothing had moved one single inch.

Braddock walked over to the window to examine the glass. "I just don't get it? We went flying, but nothing else even . . ."

Devon mumbled a few words with the echo of panic escaping from his throat.

"What?" Braddock said, turning to see Devon pointing to the corner. He followed Devon's finger and saw a strange young boy propped up against the wall, as if he had casually dropped by. Braddock just stared at the boy and noticed he was dressed in such a way that Braddock had never seen before. The boy was dressed completely in a light blue outfit, or maybe an all white outfit. He couldn't tell. Sometimes it appeared to be light gray . . . or even tan. Braddock's eyes couldn't focus on the color. He closed his eyes for a minute and then opened them again, taking a new look at the boy. He must have been about seventeen or eighteen years old.

The strange boy bore a striking resemblance to Braddock, mimicking everything about him, down to the smallest charismatic movements, but at the same time, everything about him was different. He could have been an identical younger version of Braddock . . . but not quite. Possibly his son? No. He had a rough and rustic look about him, but appeared gentle and kind at the same time. His hair was completely black and he resembled Braddock's before his hair started turning gray.

Braddock continued to gaze at the boy, as the feeling came over him that he somehow he knew him. "Who are you?" he asked in soft questionable tone.

"I . . . I don't know", the strange boy helplessly stuttered.

"He appears to be more like a drone," Devon said sarcastically under his breath to Braddock.

"Yes," the boy stated calmly. "My name is . . . Adrone . . . Adronee . . . Adrain . . . Adrian . . . Yes, that is my name. My name is Adrian!"

Braddock and Devon looked at each other in complete confusion, then turned back cautiously to the stranger.

The boy kept his eyes fixed on Braddock. "My name is Adrian, I am a reconstruction of your aura. I was born through your Auratoss system."

"What are you talking about? What Auratoss system?" Braddock asked, feeling even more puzzled.

Your machine, I came from your machine!" Adrian answered, still smiling.

Braddock felt his temperature rise, "I'm sorry, I don't permit trespassers. I'm going to ask you to leave. I have a lot of work to do!" He walked to the boy, grabbing at his arm but felt nothing. His hand went right through him. He tried again but got the same result.

"Sorry I had to do that to you," Adrian said, wiping the smile from his face. "I'm a reconstruction of your aura. Something in your machine combined with me . . . and . . . and I'm real, I guess. At least you can see me."

"I think you're just some kind of second rate magician! Now get off my property!"

"No wait!" Devon interrupted. "I believe him. I just thought of a way to prove it," Devon said, as he turned sharply to Adrian. "You said you came from the machine through something called an 'Auratoss' system—so that must mean . . ." He paused and walked over to the table, picked up the enlarged picture of the fingerprint and the pad of green ink. "Okay, I need to fingerprint you!" he said.

"Are you crazy?" Braddock shouted. "I want him out of my house!"

"You saw what happened, your hand went right through him." Devon stated.

"Okay, I'm ready," Adrian said.

Devon gave Braddock one last glance for his approval.

Braddock said nothing.

Adrian dipped his thumb into the ink and stamped it onto the paper.

"Here," Devon said, handing the paper to Braddock, "you examine it."

Braddock took the print from Devon, carefully picked up the magnifying glass, and began to glare at every green line. "Green ink is kind of hard to see, but it's the only color I have. "Just examine it," Devon commanded.

Seconds went by and Braddock slowly looked up in astonishment. "It's a match," he said, his voice barely above a whisper.

"You see," Devon said. "It all makes sense now. Somehow you constructed your aura, or at least part of your aura, into something real! Something that can be seen by the naked eye!"

Braddock was still skeptical. "How is that possible?"

"I'm not sure," Devon said, sitting down in a nearby chair. "Do you have any powers?"

"Powers?" Adrian asked, confused.

"You know, gifts, talents. Can you do anything special?" Devon said, watching Adrian's expressions.

"I am reconstructed aura in physical appearance. I am no more than I am. I can do no more than I can do."

"Ah," Braddock interrupted. "I said those words many times before I ever completed any of my inventions. If you are half an aura as you claim, your body should be very flexible. Can you touch your toes?"

Adrian bent over and placed his hands flat on the floor.

"Good, good," Braddock said, opening a small panel door on the side of his homemade machine. "Hold that position please." A small, thin, red beam of light stretched out over Adrian's body, scanning his molecular structure. "Please stand," Braddock said again.

Adrian then stood straight and tall as the light beam again scanned his entire body from head to toe.

Braddock turned to his computer and began typing some commands. "Good, that should do it!" he said, still typing. Instantaneously, the printer sped-fed the printing readout, and Braddock ripped it from the machine almost before it had finished printing. "Wow!" Braddock commented. "Your molecular structure is backwards. In the bent position the molecules in your body are spaced twice as far as in the standing position!"

"What does that mean?" Devon asked, rising from his chair.

"Well . . . the smaller Adrian were to get, the further the molecules in his body would separate until he would become nothing, or 'space' as it were. But as we now know, everything is ultimately infinite. So, theoretically, if we could collapse his molecules or 'shrink' as it were, in effect we could reassemble Adrian . . ."

". . . What? In the future?" Devon asked.

"No, right here, in this time, right now" Braddock continued.

"That would be terrific." Devon said, trying to sound thrilled, as he sat back down in his chair.

"The only thing is . . ." Braddock said, looking the readout over one more time.

Devon looked at Braddock.

"He would be microscopic. His aura molecules are as flexible as he is, so they could be separated and regrouped on a microscopic level."

Devon was dumbfounded. "Microscopic?" he said, standing.

"Right! But we would need to apply great pressure or something else to contain his elastic molecules until they rejoin."

"Microscopic?" Devon said again, still stunned.

"Absolutely!" Braddock said, handing the readout to Devon. "Just think of all the things that we could accomplish! We could examine germs and bacteria up close or you could kill viruses . . . you know, hands on! That might be the only way to destroy the common cold! Or, he could possibly grow smaller than that."

"Smaller?"

"Yeah, depending where on the scale the reassembling would take place. He could be microscopic or beyond."

"Well, let's do it! Let's get started!"

"It's not that easy. I don't have the equipment or . . . it's going to take a lot more than I've got." Braddock felt a weariness befall him and he needed time to think. 'Excuse me," he said politely.

"Where are you going?"

"I just need a few minutes. Please, make yourself at home," Braddock said, as he turned and headed toward his bedroom.

Devon shrugged and looked at Adrian who shrugged in return. "Can you grant wishes?" Devon asked.

Braddock closed the door to his room and stretched out on his bed as images raced back and forth through his mind. For several minutes he felt as if he had greater strength then Adrian. Then, an image, an idea, a plan . . . a plan that made more sense the more he thought about it. His heart raced as the idea pulsed through his brain. The seconds, minutes, and hours passed. Braddock awoke to the tapping from outside of his door.

"Yes?" he said, sitting up.

"Are you okay in there?" he heard Devon say.

"Yeah. Um, how long have I been out?"

"Three hours!"

"Three hours?" Braddock thought to himself, climbing out of bed.

Devon opened the door slowly and peered in, "I heard you analyzing figures in here and wondered if you needed any help."

"I do that in my sleep sometimes."

"Wow, in your sleep. That's a talent I need to pick up."

"It's all so clear now! I know how to shrink Adrian to microscopic proportions safely and what to achieve!"

"What? How?"

Adrian emerged into the room. "Do you mind if I talk to my new friend Braddock for a few minutes, Mr. Steinbrook?"

"Of course. I need to be going anyway, it's getting extremely late," Devon said, then turned to Braddock. "I will definitely be in touch."

Braddock smiled.

"Oh, and Adrian."

"Yes?"

"Please call me Devon."

"I will."

Devon left shutting the door behind him.

"Yes, Adrian?" Braddock asked, moving to the head of the bed and leaning his weight against the head board.

Adrian crawled onto the foot of the bed among the red velvet bedspread and crossed his legs. "It's all happening kinda fast, isn't it?"

Braddock held his pillow in his lap. "Ideas just come to me as fast as machine gun fire and I just have to act. It's the only way to get things done."

Adrian grinned because he knew Braddock was right.

"Who are you? Who are you really?" Braddock calmly spoke.

Adrian's tone became soft. "I am half of you and half of something that is unknown. I have half of your memories, like, remember the time we made that weather altering machine when you were just a kid? You know, the one that could make summer into winter and winter into summer? That's all that I can remember, what ever happened to it?"

"It blew up. I never did have much luck with my machines, they always exploded one way or another. In fact, I never even knew this last machine that I made was an Auratoss."

Both laughed. Adrian laughed loudest of all, reflecting on Braddock's attempted successes and definite failures.

"And how about the time our sister punched me in the mouth in the first grade," Braddock added. "I lost my tooth on the playground and our teacher, Mrs Phillips, had to send a note home to the Tooth Fairy because she couldn't find the tooth."

"I remember that! What do you suppose the Tooth Fairy does with all of those teeth?"

"She uses them to build her castle."

"Right."

"Braddock squeezed the pillow tighter. "I can't believe that I'm sitting here talking to myself . . . My solidified aura. Whatever or whoever separated us has done their job well, we're two different entities now!"

"Do you really think that I can shrink down and destroy viruses?" Adrian asked politely.

Braddock paused to think. "Yes, but not for a while. I will need to get more people to help me and I will need more time to sort out the details."

Adrian nodded. "I would like to do that very much! I know that it was our wish for a long time and I am willing to go for it!"

"You remember that too, huh?"

"Yes."

"Do you remember what my favorite food is?"

Adrian chuckled. "Chinese, or anything Italian!"

"Right! Are you hungry?"

"I'm famished."

Braddock led Adrian off the bed and out the bedroom door. "We'll order out, and you can sleep in the guest room until we can get Project Micro-launcher underway."

"That sounds wonderful!" Adrian confided.

2

Jaunt

Seven moths later, outside Washington D.C.

"Braddock McGee! Please come to the control room!" a voice echoed over the intercom.

"I'm sorry, I really must be going!" Braddock said, inadvertently turning from the reporter and continuing down the long white hallway.

"Is it true that this is a government conspiracy?" the reporter asked, scurrying to keep up.

"What? No!"

"Is this the plot to overthrow the government?"

"You contradict yourself!" Braddock said, entering the control room and forgetting the reporter. "Okay, everybody. What do we got?" he declared, running his fingers nervously through his hair.

"We're running self-maintenance procedures now, sir!" a nearby analyst cried out over the bustle in the room.

Braddock looked over the vast sea of computers to the large screen that beheld the image of Adrian wearing his white uniform that had one single pocket on the upper left hand corner. He was securely strapped into his chair. "Adrian? Buddy? Can you hear me?"

"I thought you weren't going to show up!" Adrian responded.

"You know me better than that."

Adrian gave a thumbs up, as an assistant helped Adrian put his helmet on.

"Dr. McGee?" an unfamiliar voice said from behind.

Braddock turned to see Dr. Gill. He had known Dr. Gill briefly back at the university while he had been working toward his Master's Degree.

"Well!" Braddock said, baring a small hug, as if in a lost admiration. "It's been a long time!"

"It has." Dr. Gill began to look quietly around the room. "Looks like you achieved your fame and fortune!"

Braddock began to chuckle. "Not just yet!"

"Dr. McGee, allow me to introduce . . ." Dr. Gill said stately.

"Please, just call me Braddock!"

"Braddock, please allow me to introduce my present colleague, Dr. Stat."

"Pleased to meet you!" Braddock said, shaking his hand.

"It's a pleasure!" Dr. Stat said. "Dr. Gill has been telling me many good things about your work. But the main reason I'm here is because I'm researching information on the human body for my thesis. And this is the strangest case involving the human body I've ever heard! Tell me more about this experiment!"

"Adrian is a very flexible aura right now, but when great pressure is applied he will be microscopic and just as solid as you and I."

Dr. Stat didn't quite know what to make of Braddock.

Braddock glanced at the large digital clock beating down the time on the far wall. "You're just in time!" We have exactly five minutes until launch!"

"Launch?"

Braddock gestured his arm over the sea of computers that were emitting a loud series of unintelligible beeps and electronic whistles. "Today we will make history! My friend Adrian is a boy of such versatility . . . that I'm going to send him to the center of the earth!"

"The center of the earth?"

"The center of the earth," Braddock repeated proudly, resting his hand on Dr. Stat's shoulder. "It will work like this: Adrian is placed in a ship we designed called the 'Drill', whereupon it will tunnel to the center of the earth where the pressure is the greatest. You've read my papers on Adrian, have you not?"

"Yes. Under pressure the molecules in his body separate and he is, in a sense, dismantled!"

"Correct! He will reach the center of the world, where the pressure will be the right density to propel him into microscopic elements; he will then be brought back to the surface. Once he arrives at point 5-7k at the speed of five hundred and sixty-five miles per hour, he should reassemble as a microscopic unit! He will then continue to the surface of the earth, where we will conduct the necessary experiments, and then the process will be reversed!"

"We are ready to begin launch, sir," the computer analyst interrupted.

"Great!" Are you ready to witness history?"

"Absolutely!" Dr. Gill answered.

"Right this way," Braddock said, motioning to a couple of vacant seats, just down the steps.

"I'm isolating the main system now," said the nearest computer operator.

The huge screen on the wall cast the image of the ship's outer hull that had the threads of a screw, and came to a giant point like a huge drill bit. It began to spin with a low, heavy whirring noise that shook the entire building.

"Maneuverability is at 7.89 and rising!"

Braddock stood transfixed, watching the boosters emit a vast, spreading plume of smoke. "Hypersonic rank?"

"Hypersonic rank, 6784.9511!"

"Sir, the Y.O.T. apparatus is oscillating!"

"By how much?"

".89!"

"We can still make a go of it!"

"Yes, sir."

The huge seven-story ship spun into a blur like a powerful tornado. The ship would lift high into the sky to pick up speed then plummet deep into the earth's bowels.

"Countdown in . . . 10 . . . 9 . . . 8 . . . 7 . . . 6 . . . 5 . . . 4 . . . 3 . . . 2 . . . 1 . . . lift off!"

"Torque this baby!" Braddock shouted.

Adrian held fast to the arm of his seat, banging his head heedlessly back and forth, as the entire cockpit erupted in violent jolts of untamed fury from the booster rockets. Adrian's head finally came to a rest from the G-force pressure. He could almost sense himself getting smaller.

"Adrian? Adrian? Do you copy? Over!"

Adrian fumbled his hand along the control panel, grasped the hand-held radio in his sweaty fingers, and drew it closer to his mouth. "This is Adrian, go ahead!" he said, listening to the loud cheering from the crowd in the control room that poured in from his radio.

"We had a gorgeous launch! You look beautiful up there!" Braddock commented, restraining the excitement in his voice.

"10-4!" Adrian echoed.

"What is your altitude?"

"Ten thousand feet and climbing. I will prepare for J-turn and descend now."

"Your rate of speed should reach eight hundred miles per hour, just before you penetrate the earth's surface, over."

"10-4!" Adrian said, feeling the force around him grow stronger. He took in a deep breath and relaxed, knowing Braddock's team would guide his ship deep into the surface by remote. He paused to reflect the day's events and was shaken by a hard jerk of the ship and realized he had broken the earth's surface and was heading straight for the center.

Adrian unbuckled himself and made his way from his seat up to his capsule. The ship rocked back and forth, throwing him against the wall. Adrian grabbed onto the guide rails tightly, feeling the ship's vibrations for that one moment when the ship took a brief pause, and he could continue. He found his capsule, which was made of an oblong plastic-like material in which he could make his transformation. Adrian typed the code word "honor" on the small keyboard that extended from the bottom end. The lid atop the capsule opened with a slow hiss. He loved that sound. He then grabbed the other side of the capsule for support and slid his thin frame into the cushions provided within the capsule's walls. The photo-eye recorded Adrian was in position, sent a message back to home base, and closed the capsule.

"Still coasting on the residual kinetic energy boost that originated in the fuel, sir!" uttered the operator. "Good!" Braddock answered.

"Outer temperature at eight hundred and four degrees!"

"Speed?"

"Nearing five hundred and sixty!"

"Increase five and prepare for transformation!"

"Yes, sir!"

The Drill continued its descent. the solid rock outside began bouncing off and melting into lava from the heat radiating from the intense friction.

"Speed, five hundred and sixty-five!"

"Transformation . . . now!" Braddock ordered, holding his breath.

The drill roared with reverberations of the sonic boom that erupted, causing the entire earth to shake. Braddock could sense the slight tremble on the hard floor beneath his feet.

"Transformation complete, he is now disassembled."

Braddock held his lips tight, daring not to breathe until Adrian had returned to the surface.

". . . At the center of the earth in . . . . 5 . . . 4 . . . 3 . . . 2 . . . 1 . . ."

"Trajectory upwards at 6375.9!" Braddock ordered, trying in desperation to subdue his racing heart.

The Drill began to shake and veer off course at an alarming speed, sending a race of fear throughout everyone at home base.

"Trajectory upwards at 6375.9!" Braddock repeated.

"Acknowledge, 6375.9 . . . has hit its orbit!"

Braddock breathed a sigh of relief, knowing the Drill had found an orbit around the molten center of the world and was now rapidly heading, on course, back to the surface. "Excel speed, and let's reassemble my friend!" he said, letting the blood flow, once again, through his tightly clenched fists.

"Speed at five hundred and closing! . . . Five-ten . . . five-twenty . . . five-thirty . . . five-forty . . . five fifty . . . five-sixty . . . five-sixty-five! . . . Transformation, now!"

Once again the floor beneath the entire room shook from the overwhelming sonic boom that catapulted Adrian into his microscopic state. A haunting hush befell the atmosphere of the entire room, as they waited anxiously for the words of their success; the moments grew longer with each passing second.

". . . Transformation complete! We've got us an amoeba!"

Braddock fell to his knees, gripped in the delight of success and watched his comrades as they leapt from their chairs with loud screams and laughter.

"Speed at seven-hundred and fifty, breaking the sound barrier!"

Again the floor shook from the vibrations of the sonic boom, followed by more cheering of undaunted success.

The analyst stared at the computer screen, typed a few more commands, and gawked at the screen again. Braddock jumped up from his knees and peered at her with a paralyzed expression. Chills ran down his spine.

The room fell silent.

"What is it?" Braddock calmly asked.

"I . . . . Uh, have no reading. We lost him after the last sonic boom."

"NO!" Braddock pleaded, turning the screen to look for himself. "What do you have?" he yelled to another analyst.

She tapped hard at her keyboard and collapsed into her chair. "He's gone," she said, staring at the floor. "The ship didn't make it through the sound barrier. That wasn't a sonic boom we heard, that was the Drill exploding."

The room filled with the sound of clicks and clacks, as people tapped away at their computers. Braddock sat down on the cold, hard, top step and listened to the chatter. A flood of memories came rushing back all at once, as he pictured his good friend Adrian, gone.

"All reports show that Adrian was point zero, zero, zero three times smaller that microscopic. He could have survived the blast, but the ship however was destroyed," another analyst said.

Braddock sat there.

3
The Battle of Rolin

Adrian calmly laid asleep dreaming of a black submarine submerging itself beneath the soft blue ocean water that gently rocked it back and forth, back and forth. Suddenly, a blinding flash of light from the explosion erupted furiously. Adrian awoke. He felt nothing to his right or left, then realized nothing was supporting his weight. He hovered for seconds, then the wind began whipping over his body as he fell at an uncontrollable rate. For a split second, ultimate fear plagued his mind, as panic set in. He began thrusting and grabbing at the air, desperate for something solid. But he felt nothing but air rushing between his fingers.

The light radiated continuously, and Adrian caught a glimpse of a bright blue sky between the clouds. He fell, disoriented, until he landed softly with a silent thud among beautiful golden grasses that swayed gently in the strange winds.

Where was he? The bizarre land had no sun in the sky, only the bright light of a large comet that left a long white tail that streaked gloriously up from the north horizon. Everything else about the daylight and the miraculous land appeared normal.

Adrian lay there in almost a dream-like state with his mind trying to search for any kind of pain. He felt fine and sat up abruptly, holding his head and trying to regain his orientation. He felt suddenly more solid; it was the strangest feeling. He looked at his hands and was surprised to see that they were shorter and thicker than they had been when he was only half solid. He gave one final shake of his head and began to observe his surroundings. He looked out on the gently rolling hills of amber plants. Braddock had once showed him a picture of a wheat field, but on examining one of the stalks closer, they appeared nothing alike. He looked out once again at the rolling waves and was soothed almost once again into a hypnotic trance, but was quickly interrupted by the faint sound of fierce music coming from the distant horizon. A bright red flag broke the serenity of the golden plants rolling into the constant deep blue sky. He desperately missed Braddock and just wanted to go home.

A line of several hundred jet-black hovercrafts geared for war, appeared over the horizon. The battle cry crisply sounded; the light glared and flickered off the smooth black paint. The soldiers, dressed in their dark blue, neatly pressed uniforms, throttled and revved the silent humming motors. And with the battle cry at its inspiring peak, they charged down the hill in full force.

Adrian froze as the troops drew nearer. The battle cry rang in his ears with a subtle enticing movement that made him want to stay and fight. But something felt terribly wrong with these men; they wore waist-length blue cloaks over their blue uniforms, but also covered their faces with a thick solid blue mask that was carved with identical black markings that gave them sinister expressions. Over their heads they sported heavy blue helmets that hung down below their ears. They resembled androids but were definitely men—all of which stood exactly the same height! Adrian just knew that he would run into them again.

A large clanging noise from behind sent Adrian spinning around to see a more unusual sight. Men on foot, wearing tattered and torn uniforms of all different faded colors, were charging from the other direction. Only two soldiers were aboard hovercrafts of their own.

Adrian was surrounded, but he showed no fear because he reasoned they were not after him, but each other. He ran hard upwind, away from his ultimate fate and reached a small hill that overlooked the terrible battlegrounds. He turned just in time to watch the fierce opponents engage in the deadly war, as they thrust into each other.

A man, in a torn, dark green uniform, stood transfixed ringing a hand-held silver bell with great pride. The soldiers aboard the solid black hovercrafts opened fire with fifty-caliber machine guns; the silver bell sailed off into the air and was lost among the golden waves of grain. Within minutes the battle was over, with nothing remaining but a few of the soldiers in blue and their black hovercrafts that drifted off in unison.

Adrian walked slowly down the hill, feeling the grasses crumble beneath his feet. He arrived at the battle scene and stepped gently over the dead and wounded bodies. Men agonized and screeched with pain, but they laid very still. A sudden movement caught Adrian's eyes. A man, wearing a tattered green uniform, jumped to his feet and without a twitch, pointed a gun directly between Adrian's eyes. He had been the man ringing the bell.

The man looked Adrian over one time and began to chuckle. "Well, well, you're no threat, are you? You can't be one of them! You aren't beef enough to be one of them!"

Adrian's gaze fell on the man's face. He was an older man, with a salt-and-pepper beard that covered most of his chubby little face; he also wore a small black hat that sat precariously on his head.

"No," Adrian stated solemnly, showing the man his hands were empty of any weapons. "I am absolutely no threat . . . I just need your help!"

The man laughed louder. "You! You are coming to me for help! My whole army just got wiped out! Don't come to me for help, my boy!"

"But, sir . . ." Adrian squealed.

"Now, now! Let's get out of here!"

"But, what about the others?!"

"The selextives will see to their medical needs later; let's just get out of here!" he said, jumping aboard the nearest hovercraft.

Adrian paused, not knowing whether to follow or not.

"Are you coming?"

"Well . . ."

"'Well' is a tactical error! A lot of men die by saying 'well'! Get on or I'll leave you!"

Adrian jumped on the craft without hesitating. He landed hard on the uncovered seats and pain shot up from his tail bone. He turned his mind's attention away from the pain by examining the hovercraft. It was an old, rusty piece of junk that needed to be resurfaced and repainted. He could see the rusty gray metal through the chips of black paint that remained. The old man fired the craft up with a loud bang. The hovercraft backfired, shooting sparks thirty feet to the rear. Adrian had second thoughts about going; he doubted that this old clunker could ever really make it to their destination.

"Hold on!" the man shouted.

"Can I ask you a question?" Adrian shyly asked.

"Make it fast!" he said, looking at Adrian, as the craft shut down.

"You seem awfully cheerful, especially after such a battle!"

"Tactics my boy, tactics! Without spirit you have no morale!" he said, turning to start the craft up again.

The hovercraft leapt forward seven feet, then came to a sharp stop without dying this time.

Adrian grabbed the back of the seat, but the immense pressure of the sudden stop pulled his fingers from the hard board and threw him to the floor.

"Here we go!" the man shouted, with this strange laughter.

Adrian wanted to go home more than ever.

The craft chugged along uneasily, and although the craft hovered three feet above the ground, Adrian could feel every bump. The craft backfired and moaned several more times, as the strange man quietly sang to himself.

Minutes passed and Adrian began to grow sick from the jolting and chugging. Holding fast to the side of the hovercraft for support, he glanced just above his unsteady fingers and beheld a small oasis of trees in their path and nothing more in this eternal sea of waving grain.

"Almost there!" the man said.

Adrian peered over the side once again and looked deeply into the small group of trees. He saw nothing.

The man sped the craft full throttle, and they were amid the trees in no time. A large gate below the hovercraft opened rapidly with deep electric howls. Adrian once again felt the falling sensation, but it was cut short with a sudden bouncing thud.

"At last, among friends!" The man sang out.

Adrian sat himself upright and glared at the solid dirt walls. The man throttled the shuttle again, and they flew down through a dark corridor that Adrian failed to see. An opening soon appeared, and Adrian sat rigidly, forgetting his shortened sickness, and gawked in wonder at an entire underground empire. The buildings reached to infinity. Being dark brown in color and rough in texture, they enclosed the small passing craft, as they made their way down a small path. The humongous structures reflected some kind of light from an unknown source that lit the enormous underground kingdom, so Adrian could see the very top of each building as well as he could its base.

Adrian noticed very few people. Every once in a while he caught a glimpse of a gentleman or lady who gave a friendly wave and a short laugh, then would carry on with their business.

The hovercraft continued on still, passing building after building, minute after minute.

"Ah," the man sighed, upon seeing a large black cave opening that lay just ahead. Nothing like being home, huh?!"

"I wish I knew."

"Yeah, that's right," the man said, looking at Adrian.

"You need my help . . . well, you don't worry 'bout nothing, we'll find out where you need to be!"

The hovercraft continued on into the pitch-black cave. Adrian noticed the lack of an echo that went along with most caves. "How high is the roof in this cave?" he asked.

"I don't really know; it's fairly high. We built this cave as a getaway! We come out here, build us a camp fire, sing us a few songs—then back to work as usual!"

At the sound of a few men cheering off in the distance, Adrian squinted his eyes and peered through the dim light. He saw the small flicker of light that approached fast as the man accelerated the craft towards the campfire that had been built.

"Well, I see you made it . . . where, uh . . . where's Tad?" one man said, as the hovercraft came to a complete stop.

"He didn't make it," the pilot said, jumping down from the craft.

The few men around the fire took a few minutes to pause and wipe a tear from their eye.

"When will this forsaken war be over?!" another man shouted, throwing his hat into the fire.

Adrian sank into his seat, not willing to disturb the mood with his presence.

"That was just a small Die-cell party," Adrian's new friend said, walking closer to his buddies.

"What did you do, capture yourself a spy?" the other man said, motioning to Adrian.

"No, this boy was just wandering around the battlefield. Says he needs our help."

"Needs our help? Hop on down here, son."

Adrian looked at the man and hopped down from the craft.

"My name's James, Ben you know, and back there is Gimmer," James said.

Adrian glanced over at Ben. "I'm afraid we weren't properly introduced."

"No, we didn't have much time to chat," Ben said, avoiding Adrian's glare.

"Well, we're all one big happy family now," James commented. "Come on over by the fire and tell us why you need our help, and I'll tell you how we can use your help."

Adrian sat down on the cold stone log and listened to the sound of artificial crickets chirping from unseen speakers hidden behind him.

"You didn't tell us your name?!" James said, in an arrogant tone.

"My name is Adrian. I was part of a project to . . ."

"You are a spy, I knew it!" James snapped.

"Sit down, James, I don't believe he's no spy!" Ben argued.

James looked at Adrian's face. "Look, I'm sorry. We're right in the middle of a war. The battle you witnessed today was A-rank . . . or, uh, Ben and his men. If the Die-cells return, I have to assemble my troops and defend this tiny planet."

Adrian couldn't believe what he was hearing! He had discovered an all new galaxy! All new life forms! He was on a microscopic planet! "How big is this planet?" Adrian asked, trying to stick to the matter at hand.

"About four hundred miles long or so," James continued.

Adrian gasped. "Why do the Die-cells want to capture a four hundred mile, inside-out planet?"

"You really aren't from around here, are you?!" James chuckled. "It's a long story."

"I'd love to hear it!" Adrian begged.

James sat down on a stone log across the way and stirred the fire. "Fifteen years ago," he said, "we elected a king by the name of Adam Tucks, who renamed the galaxy after himself. He issued an ultimatum that all laws and ordinances would henceforth be subject to his rule, as well as his posterity's. Not many people were opposed to this, including myself because government would not be a controlling power. Over the course of the next five years, there arose another force opposed to the rule that Adam laid before the people. The party, led by the powerful dictator, Diabolis [Die-a-bol-is] which stands for diabolic, or diabolical. He would insure the government took more control over the people and the laws of the land. Diabolis and his followers entered into a civil war, capturing the western portion of the galaxy. He was not happy with just being ruler and king for his short ten-year reign; he has opted to physically remove the western hemisphere from the eastern and relocate it to another area in the solar system. That is why we are at war; we are centrally located and wish to stay with the eastern Adam Force."

"Have you tried to make Diabolis retract and leave the eastern and western hemispheres as one strong unit?" Adrian stated.

"King Adam has not issued a statement as to what course of action should be taken," James quipped.

"Have any of the people, in the eastern or western galaxy, made any statements of discontent about Diabolis and his rule?"

"What are you implying, Mr. Adrian? Are you saying that the people of the Adam Galaxy are nothing more than a bunch of lazy losers who want this galaxy ripped apart?" James shouted, jumping to his feet.

"I'm not implying anything!"

"All right! All right!" Ben interrupted, "Arguing tonight won't do any good. Look, Adrian, we need your help. We don't ask much, we just need more forces to keep this great land of ours from being jolted off somewhere out into the solar system. Will you do that with us?"

Adrian sat back and took a deep breath. He would have to until he could find a way home. "Yeah . . . Yeah, I'll do my best."

"Good that's all we ask, do your best!" Ben continued, turning to James. "That should do it for tonight; let's turn in and we'll worry more about training Adrian first thing tomorrow morning."

James approached Adrian. "You have great spirit. I like you, kid! I'll tell you what, you can take my room on the third-hundredth floor of the Garnet Building, room five-zero-five! I'll make other arrangements."

"That does remind me! Where is the rest of the population? I only noticed a few people or maybe more in this fabulous luxurious city of yours."

"They boycotted their city and our retaliating movement and moved further east, those bunch of useless . . ."

"Don't say it, James!" Ben interrupted. "If you want to get in my hovercraft, Adrian, I'll show you to your building."

"My building?"

"Absolutely! We have over sixteen hundred empty buildings; everything is yours for the taking. You'll be living with two other recruits who have been staying with James for training purposes," Ben said, smiling.

"That sounds great!"

Ben reached into his pocket and pulled out a small black remote and with a single touch of a button, the fire they had been sitting around switched off like an electric light.

4

The New Recruits

"This will be your room," Ben said kindly, unlocking and opening the large white door.

Adrian stood in awe at the size of the room. The ceiling reached fifty-feet into the air, and it would take him several minutes just to walk to the other side of the room and back. Then Adrian noticed the bed and other furniture had no legs for support; they levitated motionless three feet above the ground. He sat gently on the side of the bed, and it gave a slight bounce; he bounced harder and the bed jumped five feet, and shifted across the room, and came to rest on the other wall. "Wow!" Adrian cheered, "how does it do that?" he said, examining the underside of the bed.

"This is the exact middle of our planet; things have a tendency to do that. Back when this planet was populated, this room used to rent out for one million truplets a night."

"This is great! I would like to explore the rest of your planet."

"Sounds like a good idea to me, but first I would like for you to meet your neighbors." Ben walked to the door across the room to the left and gently tapped out a small tune. The door flew open momentarily and two of the most bizarre looking men tumbled in and fell to the floor.

The first stood rather tall with a proud gawky expression, and the other, half his size, sported a large crooked hat that covered his eyes, so that all that could be seen was his flat red nose and tiny little mouth.

"Rigid formation!" Ben ordered.

The two men tripped their way to their feet and stood at attention.

"Gentlemen," Ben commanded, walking toward Adrian. "This is our new recruit, Adrian! Treat him with respect and dignity!"

Adrian felt himself swell up inside with laughter looking upon this sorry excuse for an army and leader.

"I leave you to show our new friend the ropes!" Ben continued. "Dismissed!" he said, exiting the room.

Can you believe this whole war thing?!" the tall one said as soon as Ben closed the door behind him.

"It is a little hard to believe," Adrian agreed.

"Have you ever served in the army before?" chimed in the short one

"No, I've never had the pleasure."

"Pleasure?" the two men said simultaneously, staring at each other. "You are new! Where do you come from?" asked the tall one.

"Earth."

"Earth?" said the short one, pulling his hat back to his forehead, revealing his eyes. "I've never heard of that!"

The two men walked over and sat on either side of Adrian on the bed, sending it shuffling another six feet horizontally along the floor.

"Let me introduce myself," said the taller of the two. "My name is Rhesus Turnbuckle and my little friend over here . . ."

"Hey! I'm not little!"

". . . Like I was saying, my little friend over here is Seth Biggs!"

"It's nice to meet you," Adrian responded.

"Okay, I might be short, but I'm no dreamer!"

"I'm not a dreamer, I've got plans! You make it sound like I'm some complete idiot!" Rhesus shouted.

"What are your dreams?" Adrian calmly asked.

"This whole war is a waste of time. I know . . . I know I could break the line of defense and put an end to the plans of Diabolis once and for all."

"How would you go about breaking the line of defense?" Adrian questioned.

"Look at me! Diabolis and his army would never realize I was a real threat until it was too late!"

"Rhesus? Seth said, letting his hat fall back over his eyes. "Tell Adrian your real plan, the plan that you told me earlier."

Rhesus paused, rose from the bed, and stared longingly out the window. Adrian could sense a serious change in the mood he could tell that these two men, as weird looking as they were, had deep dreams and a burning desire to change the history of that galaxy.

"It is really a matter of reaching King Adam. We have to let him know that the people do not want the galaxy divided; the people in this universe, no matter how tough or strong they appear, are nothing more than a bunch of complete wimps, who are looking out for nobody but themselves. They do fight for their homes, but they don't fight against the threat that threatens to take their homes away. Adam is a good man; he just needs to know that the people care, then he needs a man of action who can come up with a plan that will end Diabolis and his reign."

Adrian was speechless.

Rhesus turned from the window with a solemn, radiating expression. "I do believe that man is me," he said quietly.

Adrian remained silent and gave Seth a small glance, watching him slide his hat back to his forehead once again. Adrian could sense somewhere in his soul that this man could and would eventually pull it off. He turned again to Rhesus, and a huge relaxing grin spread across his face. "Do you have a plan of action?"

Seth looked concerned.

"No, but I know I can come up with something," Rhesus said.

"Then let's go!"—Adrian stopped . . . why had he said that? Why had those words been uttered from his lips? He had not meant to say them. He looked hesitantly up at Rhesus, who was standing completely mesmerized.

"You, you, mean it?" he spoke.

"Well, uh, yeah."

"Tonight?" he uttered again.

"Yeah."

"Wait a minute!" Seth argued, bringing a little bit of reality back to the moment. "You want us to go AWOL?!"

"Yeah . . . YEAH! LET'S DO IT!" Rhesus shouted, ecstatically.

"We just can't just leave!"

"Why not?"

"Because we've made a commitment to battle!" Seth shouted, rising from the bed.

"This is battle!"

"This is a dream!"

"It is a dream but it's my dream! Adrian believes I can achieve it!"

Seth paused and stepped back in thought, "I don't know."

"Don't know what?" Rhesus jumped in, taking advantage of Seth's brief moment to think. "Don't know if my plan will work, or don't know about me?"

"I . . ." Seth turned and searched Adrian for help; Adrian just shrugged and sat quietly on the bed. "I don't know if . . . you really have a plan to get us to King Adam!"

"I don't have a plan to get us there, but we will steal a craft from Ben, and succeed to our destination through the rigors of war. With nothing but our wit! Our training from James and Ben!"

"I still don't know."

"We can do it," Rhesus uttered softly, with a great strength of encouragement behind his voice.

Seth continued to ponder this momentous decision with tremendous agony. He turned away from Rhesus and stared at the floor, pacing back and forth.

"It will work. I won't let you down!" Rhesus threw out, as one last emotional boost in his favor.

"I . . . I'll do it for you." Seth mumbled under his breath, realizing he was making the biggest mistake of his life.

"Then let's go, right now!"

Seth's gaze shot to Rhesus's stern expression as his tall friend rushed to the window and flung it open.

"We go, now!" Rhesus ordered again.

Seth paused.

Rhesus wasted no time, and without giving anything a second thought, jumped head first out the window. Seth gave Adrian a fierce nod of approval, and he too disappeared out the window.

Adrian sat in total amazement, debating in his mind whether to follow or not. He gave the elegant room one last look and jumped up from the bed, sending it once again hovering to the other wall. He turned his pained mind towards the window, upped the ante, and leapt out of it, just as Rhesus and Seth had done.

Adrian closed his eyes tightly and prepared for the long falling sensation that he had felt once before. He landed shortly on the hard concrete and stumbled forward, landing hard on his face, sending loose bits of gravel between his teeth. He sat up rubbing his chin just in time to see Seth and Rhesus scamper over the edge of the building onto the next roof, and continue on at a rampant rate.

Adrian staggered to his feet, brushed himself off, and followed after his new friends as if nothing had happened. He leapt over the edge of the building and bolted at a die-hard pace, soon catching up with the others. The threesome dodged over, up, down, from flat roof to flat roof like a well-rehearsed dance. Adrian looked out in amazement at the stunning beauty of the city, as his feet carried him instinctively over the rough, hard obstacles.

Rhesus soon came to a stop at a small area of water ten foot square.

"What do we do, now?" Adrian asked, coming up from behind.

"Down," Rhesus replied.

"*Down?* Adrian thought to himself.

In the middle of the ten-foot concrete area of water arose a thick brown pole, around which floated a thick square platform, big enough for four men. Rhesus made a small leap onto the platform and began to strap himself, in a standing position, to the pole on the far side of the platform with a red safety buckle. Seth leapt across the water as well and fastened himself in.

"Are you coming or not?" Rhesus yelled, exasperated.

Adrian didn't worry how deep the water was or what this contraption was capable of doing He too leapt to the platform and fastened himself securely into the buckles.

"Hold on to the handles, tight!" Seth encouraged.

Rhesus flipped open the clear plastic lid to a watertight box that enclosed a small computer. He typed in the numbers 4-1-2 and closed the box securely. The platform began to slowly turn in a circle around the pole.

Adrian looked across in puzzlement at Rhesus.

"Hold on!" Rhesus said, smiling, as the platform began to pick up speed.

The four corners of the platform came within four feet of the outer edges of the concrete pond. The water began to swirl clockwise in an even steady pattern of rhythm with the platform. Adrian looked somewhat fearfully into the depth of the dark water as the platform picked up more and more speed. He clenched tighter to the handles as wind from below whirred over his body, sending the platform into a full blown spin. He gasped for his breath, watching everything around him become a solid blur of color and motion.

The platform picked up more speed still and plunged deep into the dark spinning water, sending a solid wall high above their heads. The whirlpool thrust the three friends continuously downward. Things seemed to level off, at least from Adrian's point of view, and he gained enough consciousness to speak clearly enough for Rhesus and Seth to understand him. "Where are we ... what ... what is this thing?"

"This is our waterways system. We are spinning through a whirlpool until we reach the ground floor!" Rhesus shouted above the rumbling of the water.

"Can this device go in any direction?"

"No only vertical!" Seth responded.

"*You mean vertigo*," Adrian said to himself.

The passageway to the ground floor continued on, spinning uncontrollably, with just an occasional mist of water felt. Adrian glanced down and noticed the square platform now took a circular shape, due to the rapid spinning. He began to slowly enjoy the ride and didn't want to see it come to an end. All at once he began to sense a shortage of air and began to gasp and wheeze. A sudden burst of light suddenly hit him, with a gust of cool, crisp, clean air. They had made it through the tunnel, and Adrian turned his gaze to the water that roared overhead, clinging to the walls with centrifugal force. A clear see-through hatch electronically closed, and he watched as the water swirling above slowly, but peacefully, came to a silent rest.

Adrian unbuckled the latch to his safety belt and was swiftly whisked away in a dizzy spin down the street and into the wall of a building. He slid down the wall into a heap with his mind still spinning the world around him into an almost unconscious state. He awoke a minute later to the sound of uncontrollable laughter.

"What would we do without the new guy, eh, Biggs!" Rhesus spurted out between epileptic jolts of laughter.

"Ha, ha! Yeah!" Seth laughed in agreement.

Adrian scowled. "Let's just go, all right?"

Rhesus and Seth gave one last amused chuckle and scampered off again. They soon came to a large covered garage which held hovercrafts of all shapes and sizes, none of which were new or especially eye catching.

"There it is!" Rhesus called out, running to the craft. "It's called a ziere craft!"

Adrian choked. The small craft was in worse shape than Ben's hovercraft.

"Wait a minute!" Seth called out.

"What?" Rhesus said, stopping.

"Something's wrong! I have the feeling we're being followed."

Rhesus looked around. "Well, I don't see anyone. Let's just get out of here!" He jumped into the craft, switched it out of idle hover, and into gear. "Oh, no!" he said, hitting the control panel in anger.

"What's wrong?" Seth asked, jumping into the back.

"It's not kickin' in!" Rhesus said, trying it again.

"What if we took another craft?" Adrian said, also jumping into the craft.

"We can't"

"Why not?"

"This is my craft! It was confiscated by our division of Adam Force."

"You told me this was Ben's craft!" Adrian said.

"So, I lied!" Rhesus said, hitting the controls again. "Hop out, Biggs, and see what's wrong with this thing!"

Seth jumped from the craft and opened the rear hatch. "Looks like a mess of wires and metal rods to me."

"Oh, come on! We don't have time for this," Rhesus said, hitting the controls once again. He jumped down, looked at the mess, and spotted the problem right away. "The master rod is not receiving a spark! Great, where am I going to get a spark!"

Rhesus heard a noise behind him and remembered what Seth had said about his suspicion that they were being followed. He raised both of his hands into the air and slowly turned around. Standing there innocently was small girl, no more than eight years old, with long dark hair and big brown eyes. Rhesus dropped his hands. "What are you doing here?" he asked the small girl politely.

"Following you!" she said alertly, placing her hands on her hips in a stern matter, "I want to join the Adam Force!"

"You want to join the Force?" Rhesus said, smiling at the thought. He then noticed the red sweater that the small girl wore over her dress and had an idea. "You know, we might be able to use your services after all."

"Yeah!" she said excitedly.

"Yeah! can I borrow your sweater for a minute?"

The small girl slipped it off, still smiling ear to ear. Rhesus took the sweater from the girl, then looked over at Seth. "When I yell, 'now', you start the craft up."

Seth nodded and jumped back into the craft with Adrian.

Rhesus wadded the sweater up and rubbed it against his head, making his hair stand on end. He placed his index finger near the end of the master rod. "Now!" he shouted. Seth threw the switch, just as a small static pulse of blue electricity shot out from Rhesus's finger.

The craft rumbled a little, then roared with a loud hum. Rhesus smiled with content and kneeled down to the little girl. "Thank you so much! You have helped the Force more than you will ever know!" he said, handing the girl her sweater back.

The little girl giggled with delight. "Your hair looks funny!"

Rhesus chuckled in return and gave the little girl a pat on the back. "You need to go home now and help your mother; she must be awfully worried about you."

The girl gave another smile that filled Rhesus's heart, then turned and skipped away.

"All right!" Rhesus shouted. "Let's move it out, troops!"

"Since when did we elect him our leader?" Seth uttered silently to Adrian.

"I heard that, Biggs!"

"Well, we don't want that!" Seth retorted.

Rhesus ignored Seth's response and manned to the controls that levitated the hovercraft up and out of the garage.

5

Deltena

The ziere craft leapt from the protection of the underground city and cast its long shadow along the eternal field of golden foliage.

Rhesus throttled the craft in a straight line for the horizon, but instead of maintaining a steady course that followed the curvature of the tiny planet, Adrian found himself thrust out into deep space. He reflected deeply on the lessons that Braddock had taught him about the powers needed to exit the atmosphere and the extreme hazards of deep space if not properly suited. Adrian asked about these hazards as well as others.

"Ha, ha," Rhesus stated. "Such a thing would only be possible if there wasn't any adequate air to breathe."

"So you have plenty of breathable air?" Adrian asked.

"Everywhere! And as for your question about lifting through the planet's atmosphere, this little baby is a boosted craft! When this baby was brand new, the propulsion on this thing could blow away a whole herd of comadones!"

"Wow," Adrian said, taking a deep breath and sitting back against the hard, uncomfortable seat. He relaxed and turned his gaze up to the heavens. The sky and surroundings were dark with the tiny flicker of light that emitted from the stars in the distance, very similar to the night sky over Braddock's house.

"Do you have the fledlocks in position?" Seth asked, examining the control panel.

"Yes, don't worry."

"I have to worry; if they find out we've gone AWOL, they'll try to find us for sure. And I don't think this contraption can do more than two knots an hour."

"This 'contraption' will do just fine! We have a huge jump on them. They won't find out anything until morning."

Adrian ignored the conversation and continued to stare out into the dark night sky. "Where are we headed now?" he asked.

"Deltena!" Rhesus responded stiffly, making sure there was not a deviation of course. "It's an old trade planet, two hours straight ahead. We'll need to stop there to get supplies and weapons—the only thing is, it two hours into the western territory."

"We're entering Diabolis's kingdom?" Adrian asked alertly, sitting up straight.

"We entered Diabolis's kingdom five minutes ago. Your life's been on the line since your asked your last question."

The craft continued steadily on course for a couple of hours, when Adrian beheld the immense maroon and bluish planet there before him. The slow craft entered the atmosphere and drew nearer to the surface.

"This is Deltena, huh? Adrian said.

"Yes, we're unauthorized, so keep your eyes and ears open at all times," Seth said, glancing to the left and right.

They soon reached the rocky surface without a sign of civilization to be seen. Just rocks of soft purples, pinks, and pastel greens.

"So, are we supposed to be looking for a city?" Adrian asked.

"Yeah, it's on the other side of that fog," Rhesus added.

Adrian looked at the distant white fog that set in between the small hills. "What's the name of the city?"

"Rylo, I believe, or something like that."

Without warning, the ziere craft spun around, backfired, and fell with a thud to the ground. Adrian felt the hard jolt on the back of his neck as he was thrown suddenly from the craft.

Rhesus jumped to his feet in a rage of total anger, and quivering in disgust, hauled off and gave the craft a swift, hard kick. "YOU WORTHLESS PIECE OF USELESS SCRAP!!!" he shouted, reaching over and ripping off knobs from the control panel.

Seth and Adrian grabbed Rhesus and threw him to the rocky ground, sending him rolling in a cloud of dust. He came to rest a few feet away on his back.

"Control it!" Seth yelled.

Rhesus paused and once again stumbled his way to his feet. "Forget it! Leave the piece of junk here! I don't need it!" he said, dusting himself off and turning in a fury toward the fog.

"At least it got us here," Seth said to Adrian.

"True," Adrian stated, looking at the craft one last time, then hurrying to catch up with Rhesus.

As they drew closer to the fog, Adrian felt a sudden chill that began to nip at his skin and bite his ears. The cold began to intensify and freeze even the deepest part of his body, sending his arms and legs almost into uncontrollable convulsions to exude heat. His teeth began to chatter in rhythmic tones; then he realized a bizarre phenomenon. As he breathed out, the steam from his breath formed a slight condensation and trickled to the ground.

"I . . . I . . . think we'd better walk closer together to conserve heat," Seth suggested.

"I'm fine," Rhesus argued. "Let's just continue," he said, with anger trembling from his voice.

Seth and Adrian walked shoulder to shoulder as they entered the thick fog. Adrian parted the fog with his hand, realizing it was a solid as cotton candy. Water droplets had frozen and clung together in midair. It was the oddest feeling that he had ever experienced. He tried in desperation to grab the fog in his hands, but it would melt at his touch, form water droplets, fall, then re-freeze.

The small party continued on through the fog, with the small beams of ice beating wildly against their faces, almost numbing them into a frozen state. Adrian couldn't see more than two inches in front of his face. He felt Seth against his shoulder and hoped he knew the way, as he continued to push the thick fog aside.

The ice gave a pleasant crackling sound as they continued. Adrian could hear Rhesus five feet straight ahead and doubted he was enjoying this fog as much as he was. The ice cracked louder beneath his feet, and he noticed a vast rainbow from the light penetrating the ice crystals off to his right.

Seth paused, and Adrian took the opportunity to rub his face from the mind numbing cold. His finger felt the ridges of ice that had formed on his day growth of whiskers. Seth slowly began to walk straight ahead, then began veering to the right.

"Do you know the way?" Adrian asked, as his mouth filled and he choked on the tiny particles of ice.

Seth mumbled an inaudible jumble of sounds that Adrian barely heard and hardly understood. He just followed Seth and prayed he knew where he was going.

The fog seemed endless, and Adrian drew colder and colder by the minute. He felt a tremor of apprehension. *When is this going to end?* his mind argued.

He pressed on, his pace growing slower and slower with each passing minute. He tried once again, while parting the fog, to catch a glimpse of Rhesus.

Adrian could feel the curvature of the land beneath his feet, as they quickened the pace over and around small hills of rocky ground. His feet ached, his hands had lost all sensations and touch, but they continued on and on.

The air began to freeze his lungs with each breath that he took in, and it felt as if his lungs were filled with ice. The fog parted and the glare of the sun burned his eyes. He squinted with agony and collapsed in complete frozen exhaustion.

"You've got to keep going!" Seth ordered. "You've got to reach the warmer climate, just a bit farther!" He said, dragging Adrian along the hard ground.

Adrian continued to shiver, letting the sudden warmth overtake him ever so slowly. He began to regain the sensation of touch in his hands; he moved his fingers and placed them against the ground, stopping Seth from dragging him any further.

"Are you okay, now?" Seth asked.

Adrian didn't answer. He pressed his hands against the ground, giving him enough leverage to return to his feet.

You look awful!" Seth said, in his light-minded attitude, knocking small chunks of ice from his hat. He took hold of Adrian's arm to help steady him.

"Rylo is just a bit farther; by the time we get there, you should be warmed up."

Adrian limped off, looking ahead through his frozen eyes, trying to focus on the outline of the city that was a complete blur some distance away.

They soon came to the outer limits of the rustic village and parted the crowed of the most unusual creatures that any one had ever seen. Adrian had regained his composure and was very appreciative of the warmth, especially that given off by one or two of the strange creatures that sported no hair. Aliens and life forms from all different species crowded and pushed their way through the overpopulated small town buying, selling and trading all kinds of unique items for other items or large coins.

Adrian found this ordeal as captivating as the moment when he first met Braddock. One of the creatures stood seven feet high or more, with long brown tangled hair; he barked an angry howl of disgust at one small vender that apparently demanded the large coins to be returned. Another small gray creature rode a vander bike that expelled a solid green laser light propulsion system from the rear. Cutting Adrian off, he swerved and collided with a humanlike creature that wore a brown robe fastened around his shoulders.

A barredeer, which is a dark-skinned slug creature, slithered his way through the crowd to aid anyone hurt. The man with the waving brown robe crawled to his feet and watched as the barredeer confronted the small gray rider, as he picked up and once again started his vander bike. The barredeer growled in frustration and grabbed the small rider around the torso. The rider squealed in pain and tried in desperation to pry himself loose from the barredeer's lock tight grip The human like creature pleaded to the large oozing slug and pointed out that no real damage had been done.

The crowd parted and Adrian witnessed a large group of soldiers run in, wearing the dark blue uniforms and masks that he had seen before. They quickly surrounded the large barredeer without saying a word. Adrian immediately recognized the soldiers as the Die-cells that had invaded the small planet of Rolin, in which James and Ben had lived.

"Die-cells!" Seth gasped, pulling his hat over his face and sneaking into the gathering crowd.

Adrian stood transfixed and watched as the Die-cells pushed probes into the flesh of the barredeer's hand. Electric impulses surging through his hand, forced the barredeer to turn the gray rider loose. The barredeer grabbed his wrist and tried to squeeze his strong muscles harder, but it was no use, the gray rider fell from his powerful grip and landed on his vanderbike. The Adrian gasped in horror as the Die-cells painfully ended the life of the barredeer as wall as the gray rider, then wistfully turned and pursued the fleeing humanlike man as he darted in terror through the crowd.

Adrian reflected on what he had just seen, as Seth grabbed him from behind. "Come on," Seth cried silently, "let's find Rhesus!"

Adrian tried to keep his eye on Seth as he darted behind this creature and that, in a dead run. He realized that if he ran into or knocked any of these creatures over, it might mean his life. His eyes scanned his obstacles sporadically as he carefully maintained his balance until he followed Seth into a clear opening.

"He's in there!" Seth shouted, darting into a large building.

Adrian followed and found himself amid an elaborate setting of finely crafted tables and furniture, which seemed out of place for such an old, broken down building. Two men appeared out of the shadows and approached Rhesus. Even their smirks did not sit well with Adrian, but he did admire the fine white suits they wore.

"Arnraool mecanist.," The first man said, with an air of unsettling politeness. *"Riva alast mon ernsti?"*

Rhesus turned to Seth. "Can you translate?"

Seth pondered the question. "It sounds like Rebic. I can certainly try . . . . *Envistmon arenti gost flipist?* (We are looking to buy or trade).

"*Rabacliso engooten mano!* (Then we are your men) *Kalicen bigotso Corvolo en sti Yashmi!*"

"They say their names are Corvolo and Yashmi," Seth sated to Rhesus.

"*Talia mis urstanten?*"

"They also want to know what our needs are."

Tell them we need a ship, weapons and supplies," Rhesus responded.

"*More ret gask de ship . . .*" Seth asked, getting interrupted.

"*Plagunslithi gert un Rylo blas en ship?*" (How did you arrive at Rylo without a ship?)

"*Begoto ziere craft!*" Seth answered politely.

The two men broke out in laughter and looked over the three strange travelers mockingly, "*Begoto ziere craft . . . ha ha ha . . . enplato plagunslithi gert un Rylo plagdee henita opwer thet une Die-cells!*" (There is only one way to arrive at Rylo on a boosted craft, and that's to steal one from the Die-cells).

"*Uh uh untide omee ot walatee!*" (Uh . . . uh . . . my friend is a corporal), Seth stuttered through his lie.

"Well?" Rhesus asked, impatiently. "Will they give us a ship?"

Corvolo took a long pause. "*Hathue en halaton a ship.*" (I will sell you a ship!) "*Vanameere! Vanameere!*" (Thank you, thank you), Seth said with a smile.

"*Deatsore van ship geetia?*" Corvolo stated.

"He wants to know what type of ship we want."

Rhesus wasted no time answering. "Tell him we need a Van Guard!"

"*Van Guard?!*" Corvolo shouted, hearing this.

"*Oplee an hestered un Die-cells!*" (Only the best for the Die-cells), Seth said humbly.

Corvolo questioned this strange crew and wondered what Seth was thinking under that big strange hat. "*Remoree cheen yore?*"

"Do we have any money?" Seth asked Rhesus shyly.

Rhesus stood firm. "Tell him they will receive any and all payments after we see the ship!"

"*Blahae ven ists ifmore rhen de ship!*" Seth recited.

"*Till undre hooder!*" Corvolo stated.

"He said they'll need more!" Seth repeated.

"Tell them we will also throw in the ziere craft!" Rhesus said, still standing firm.

"The ziere craft? Seth asked, a bit puzzled.

"Tell them!" Rhesus ordered again.

"*Sarth foe doon veer ziere craft!*" Seth said with a fake smile.

Corvolo paused again, which gave Seth an uneasy, weary feeling. "*Ayn panero goth jist ships!*" (I will show you to our ships).

"*Wit wasen deen weapons un eats?*" (What about weapons and food?) Seth asked, bowing his head politely.

"*Thit* dwerd *weapons un eats val thertive gie stwarq de Van Guard!*" (The weapons and food will be provided if you purchase the Van Guard).

"*Vanameere! Vanameere!*" (Thank you, thank you).

"*Geem firn at veeder fanner it ships, deff den ature Yashmi ret attroon de ziere craft!*" (Follow me to the ships, and Yashmi will retrieve your ziere craft).

"*Gether fereen te wastarn fog!*" (It is on the other side of the fog), Seth said, now beginning to fear for his life. Once they found the craft in a wrecked heap, it would surely be over.

Corvolo led them to a nearby ship yard and showed them a smaller model spy cruiser. The small cruiser was similar to many Rhesus had seen before and had grown accustomed to. It appeared to have served in many, many battles and had apparently lost.

"Tell them we want a Van Guard in better than average condition, or we'll take our business elsewhere," Rhesus said, covering his frustrated tones.

"I'll see what I can do," Seth said, "*Moochague mine def Van Guard, mis stedunt goth ven histeem!*"

Corvolo shrugged in arrogant confusion. Rhesus put his hand to his chin, looked Corvolo over to call his bluff, then walked away.

"*Malameeen!*" Corvolo shouted.

Rhesus didn't know much of the rebic language, but he knew that word meant 'stop'.

"*Temusti raolia panero goth jist Van Guard!*" (All right, I'll show you to the Van Guard).

Rhesus smiled cunningly, then turned and faced Corvolo with a look of concern. Corvolo pulled his transmitter out of his pocket and held it tightly to his lips. "*Myan eldst en Van Guard!*" (Bring around the Van Guard). He then slipped the transmitter back into his pocket and kept his eyes locked on Rhesus until the ship made a thundering appearance from behind the building.

Adrian had pictured in his mind a huge state-of-the-art monster to appear, what with all the noise it had made and all the commotion it had stirred in his friends. But he stood bewildered that the ship itself was very small. The ship appeared gray to almost tan or brown, with a small highlight of gold that only appeared when the ship hit a certain light. The ship rocketed toward them, hovered, and lulled to a quiet hum. A side panel slowly opened, revealing the luxurious, well-armed innards that sent Adrian fleeing inside out of curiosity.

"I'd like to take it for a test drive," Rhesus said.

"Melan vu enst dreet minst at arue demore," Seth repeated.

"Restern avue men ater fonia alat fret ungerd." (You can sit in it, but no test drive).

"No good," Seth said to Rhesus.

Rhesus smiled graciously, broke the untrusting interlocking glare from Corvolo, and walked up the ramp into the ship, followed by Seth. Rhesus knew every inch of most Van Guards, and this ship appeared no different. He took his seat in the soft black leather cushion that gave a satisfying burp of air and adjusted snugly to his weight.

"Now tell me how we're going to pay for this?" Seth asked.

"We're not," Rhesus said, looking over the console.

"Oh, come on! Not again! We're going to have both sides of the Adam Galaxy after us! Well, not me, not this time!"

Rhesus threw a switch that immediately closed the door with a metallic bang, before Seth could make his escape down the platform.

"That's just great! That's just great! You don't even know what you're doing! Seth argued.

"I know what I'm doing," Rhesus said calmly, ignoring Corvolo's faint cries that faintly seeped in from the outside. "Now sit down and help me navigate this thing!" he ordered.

Seth reluctantly sat in the other seat to the right. "I can't believe I'm doing this! I CAN'T BELIEVE I'M DOING THIS!" he said angrily, hitting the console.

Rhesus paid him no mind as he had before and throttled the hyper sonic outer boosters.

Corvolo clenched his hands tightly over his ears and fell to his knees in the heavy dust storm the Van Guard stirred up. He held his breath and lowered his head in an attempted to avoid the small rocks that pelted his body with sharp blowing pains. When the dust had finally settled, Corvolo opened his eyes to see that the ship was gone.

6

Communication

"Braddock... Braddock," a quiet voice said with a comforting whisper of deep-felt compassion.

Braddock's mind raced with pulsing anxiety, as he sat in a hopeless haze of doubt at the loss of his friend Adrian. He breathed a heavy sigh and continued to stare at the reflection of overhead light that glimmered steadily from the white shiny tile.

"Braddock," the voice said again.

Braddock snapped out of his daze and realized the buzzing commotion that had filled the room, as all his associates continued their search for his lost friend.

"Braddock... are you okay?"

Braddock recognized that voice and quickly turned and looked up to see Devon, "Devon!" Braddock shouted, embracing him.

"What happened?" Devon asked.

"We lost him. I don't know how," Braddock quivered.

"Can you revert back to the last computer reading?"

"I don't know what's being done... I lost it."

"That's okay—take it easy," Devon said, watching his friend begin to shake. He looked around the room. "Have we got any reading on Adrian's ship yet?" he cried out.

"Not yet!" an assistant shouted.

"I do—I got it!" cried another. "I just picked up the coordinates off c.o.dox 102!"

"That can't be right!" argued yet another assistant. "That would put him somewhere under the United States Capital Building. That's almost four hundred miles off course. We would have certainly heard something if they had felt the explosion over there!"

"I'm not feeling well," Braddock spoke, "let's go back to my office."

Devon took his arm, and gently led him down the hall, and in through the small brown door that read: Braddock McGee, Lieutenant Program Manager.

Braddock collapsed on the stylish red couch and painfully rubbed his forehead. "I'm sorry, Devon . . . it's been a long time."

"Too long."

"It's been what—five years?"

"Something like that—the last time we met, I was a standing reference for your proposal hearing before the Itinerary Science Committee."

"Did you ever find the bank robber you were looking for ten years ago?"

Devon chuckled. "Yeah, six months after you received the grant, they found the guy living in Mexico—the fact he was still robbing banks gave him away."

"What have you been doing since? Are you still with E.R.T.?"

"Oh, yeah. They promoted me to sales. Ten more years and I can finally retire!"

"Good, good, glad to hear that, congratulations!"

Devon smiled his impeccable grin. "Thank you."

"Braddock McGee!" A voice interrupted over the telephone intercom.

"Yes?"

"Mr. Turner is on his way to see you."

"Thank you." Braddock looked at Devon. "They must have found Adrian."

Mr. Turner, the chief investigator, entered the room and shuffled through a small stack of papers with a precarious look of discernment. "We have learned that the ship and point of explosion was, in fact, on course and scattered debris for as far away as four hundred miles. If Adrian did survive the blast, he is located exactly under the United States Capital Building."

"How did this happen?" Braddock asked.

"The fact needs further investigation, but we believe the main oxygen tank ignited by some means and caused the bottommost part of the hull to explode and expel ninety-five percent of the debris off course. Adrian's capsule was expelled the farthest by the way the Drill twisted during disruption; this of course was five minutes and thirty-three seconds after he was transformed into his microscopic state."

"Is that all?" Braddock said, dropping his head sadly.

"for now, we are ninety two percent sure that it is the location where Adrian came to stop."

"Thank you, that will be all. Let me just have a few more minutes with my friend," Braddock said, looking up and wiping his tear-stricken face.

"Yes sir; if you need anything, don't hesitate to call."

"I will."

Mr. Turner left the room, and Braddock turned his attention to Devon. "I just wish I knew if Adrian were dead or alive. He was a part of me, you know."

Devon nodded his head, then began to think. "Ten years ago," he said, "when you tried to escort him from you house, your hand went through his arm. Does he still have those capabilities?"

"I don't know; that was the first and last time he ever did that kind of thing. I'm not even sure if he knows how to do that if he wanted to. Besides, he would have been too disoriented to do it after the crash."

"Have you tried to make any kind of communication with him?"

"After he made the transformation, it wouldn't have worked. There is no way we could make any kind of microscopic communication system; we just don't have that kind of technology."

"I think you can do anything."

Braddock smiled. "I wish."

"Exactly how big is he?"

"Thirty million times smaller than microscopic."

Devon paused for thought and got the icy chill of a good idea. "You know, back when I first met Adrian, he mentioned to us that he was from the Auratoss system and he was part of your aura. Now, if this is true, maybe you could reach him by some other means, say, telekinetic energy, or the like."

Braddock's eyes grew wide with anticipation. "You know . . . you know . . . that might just work!"

Devon felt his chest swell with pride, but he felt even better that he could cheer up his fiend.

Braddock arose from the couch, with his mind still buzzing. "But, it's going to take more than that! We really have no way of harnessing telekinetic power, unless . . . something like sound was added, but with sound it wouldn't really be telekinetic then, would it?"

"I don't know. What would the range be?" Devon asked.

"I guess it would be indefinite! I mean we pray don't we, and God might be a million miles away, right!"

"I guess."

"Yeah, I had heard once that sound itself might be fifty million times smaller than microscopic, but sound itself has very little range at all. So, if I were to combine the two then Adrian, being thirty million times smaller the microscopic could definitely hear it, but how would I combine the two without sound bringing the telekinetic energy to a halt?

"—Do you want me to escort you back to your lab?"

"Absolutely . . . there is no way I'll be able to sleep tonight!" he shouted, running out of the office.

"I can tell," Devon thought to himself, picking up a laptop that Braddock might need.

Devon and Braddock drove for some time, reflecting and discussing the events that had taken place over the last five years. Devon recognized Braddock's house immediately and pulled into the driveway.

"Just as I remember it," he said.

"Yeah, it doesn't get any better than this."

The weeks to come unfolded like minutes and seconds, days into nights and nights into days. Braddock and Devon worked together diligently, agonizing over one painful mistake and utter defeat after another. The entire project moved very slowly, and Braddock neglected almost everything else in his life. Tunnel vision and anxiety began to show on his face; his bones began to grind and ache, but he continued on. Devon ran errands and helped whenever he could, but Braddock controlled the reigns.

Devon stayed in the small guest room and was awakened one morning to the fact that Braddock had been awake all night and had put the last finishing touches on the project. "What . . . what is it?" Devon sleepily commented, coming out of a deep, restful sleep.

"Get up and follow me."

Devon stumbled from the bed, slithered into his clothes without remembering doing it, and staggered into Braddock's work room. "Yeah, it looks the same as yesterday," he said, scratching his head.

"Yeah, it looks the same as yesterday, but the only difference is . . . it works!"

Devon snapped out of his daze. "It works?!" he almost shouted.

"Yeah! I thought I should wake you so you could see it work."

"Well yeah you should wake me!" Devon said, sarcastically.

"All right! Here we go!"

Devon could see Braddock already had the main computer fired up. He stared blankly at the screen, viewing the virtual metamorphosis on the brightly lit space occupied by elementary shapes and primary colors that enhanced the pixel and coaxial lines with simple geometric construction.

"Brain waves are at a far higher, almost nonexisting frequency. I managed to combine the lower frequency of sound by upping it by almost eight thousand

and seven decibels, lowering the frequency of brain waves six hundred times, so that they sort of met in the middle," Braddock said.

Devon was amazed. "Wait a minute, if you made the pitch of sound higher by eight thousand and seven decibels—I mean, that's enough to blow the world apart."

"Only if you were to attach the speakers."

"You have to attach the speakers—that's what develops the frequency—without it you have . . ."

". . . Have what?"

"Well, just a reading, I guess."

"Right!" Braddock said, sitting at the computer. "That's where the program I formatted comes in," he said, tapping on the screen. "I wrote a program called Iabex; it takes the information form both frequencies, without actually producing the sound itself, and combines them into one."

"Okay, that sounds reasonable, but how do you reach Adrian?"

"That was the hard part! Under normal circumstances, say I was trying to reach you, with this new technology I could reach you anywhere in the world; but with Adrian I had to apply the same idea that I had when I shrunk him: I had to apply pressure by speeding the combined frequency up, then adjusted the pitch control, so it didn't sound like an intoxicated chipmunk."

"If, in fact, Adrian *is* under the United States Capital Building, how do we get this frequency to him so he can hear it?"

"Well, sometimes you have to use old technology. I had to use the old telephone pole theory, not with wires per se, but with periodical boosters. Telekinetic energy is indefinite, but I weighed it down with sound waves, so It could really only make small leaps."

"When do we transmit?" Devon said, with rapidly growing anticipation.

"Right, now!" he said, pointing to a smaller obsolete computer that sat a few feet away. "You get on that one, and when I say 'now', we will type the command 'i-o-m-e-x-1-0-1' simultaneously!"

"Iomex 101." Devon repeated, to be sure he had heard Braddock correctly.

"Yes, iomex 101."

Devon took his place at the computer and awaited further instructions.

"Okay . . . Now!"

Braddock and Devon's fingers slid across the keyboards musically, until the code had been completed. Braddock stood, and placed an awkward bolted mess of wires and metal probes on top of is head, and returned to his seat.

"Is that supposed to be a hat?" Devon implied, kicking himself for not being able to conceal his laughter.

"Don't laugh, all inventions are rusty at first," Braddock said, throwing the main switch that completed the circuit and sent a rush of electricity pulsing through the miles of circuitry that laid out to the left of the computer—so that it appeared to be alive.

Idly, Devon wondered if this impressive show would truly work, as he watched Braddock lean forward into a microphone. To Devon, he appeared to be a DJ at a radio station—only with a very impressive hat.

Braddock placed a set of head phones to his ears and began to speak softly. "Come in, Adrian, do you copy? Adrian, do you copy?" Adrian, do you copy?"

Nothing happened.

Braddock tried again, "Adrian, do you have a copy?"

"Anything?" Devon commented.

"No. Make sure the boosters are functional; they should have a readout of 106943-02 on that other computer."

Devon peered at the screen. "106943-01."

"01?" Braddock questioned.

"That's what it says."

"Are you sure you're reading it right?"

"I'm positive. Are you sure you're not forgetting to do anything?"

"I'm sure—" He then paused and looked at his thumb. "Well, ha ha, I, uh, forgot to place my fingerprint on the plate. That will shunt my physical information code across the network to reach Adrian."

Devon said nothing and watched the computer's reading: "Information access received."

"All right! Now we're getting somewhere!" Braddock cheered. "Adrian, do you have a copy?"

The computer began to grind as it processed the new information and rolled the unique combination of telekinetic energy, sound, and Braddock's physical aura into bits and expelled them from the house, leaping through a cellular network of thirty two boosters Braddock had place illegally atop various telephone poles.

"Adrian do you have a copy?" he said again, sending another pulse of information from the house.

* * *

The Van Guard glided through the darkness of space and time. Adrian sat within and watched Rhesus control the magnificent ship, sitting in one of three main seats behind the console, his face illuminated by the bright green instrument lights. His head began to spin, and a sudden sharp pain swelled dramatically from the base of his neck to the frontal lobe. The pain subsided as soon as it had begun, and Adrian's vision grew blurry—then eased as well.

The image of Braddock etched a crystal-clear vision in his brain, as if he were sitting next to him and began to speak. "Adrian—copy?"

Adrian turned his gaze to the stars outside the ship as they began to melt into one huge lit mass.

"Are you alright?" he heard Seth ask.

"My vision is just a little blurry, that's all," he uttered, turning his attention once again to the image of Braddock that cast a holographic picture on the stars in the background that had reassembled into proper shape.

"Adrian, do . . . a copy?"

"What?" Adrian responded.

"What?" Seth asked.

"Nothing," Adrian said, turning to Seth. The holographic image of Braddock now superimposed over Seth's face.

"Are you sure you're alright?"

"I . . . . I . . ." Adrian stuttered as shock began to set in. "I am seeing the image of my friend Braddock over your face."

"Your friend Braddock?"

"—do you have a copy?"

"YES!!" Adrian shouted to both questions.

The image of Braddock began to cheer like a ringing in both ears. "We did it! We did it!" It echoed.

"Did what?" Adrian inquired.

"Can you still see the image of your friend?" Seth asked.

"Yes."

"Adrian, listen to me closely," Braddock echoed again. "I need you to close your eyes tightly and focus on my image."

"I need to focus on Braddock," Adrian said, relaying the message to Seth, then closing his eyes.

"Concentrate, can you see me clearly?"

"Yes, you appear in 3-D."

"Great, it worked better than I imagined."

"How are you doing this?" Adrian asked.

"It's a long story . . . I'm just glad to see you alive!"

"What happened to me? How did I get here?"

"You completed the microscopic transformation, but the Drill was destroyed on its ascent back to the surface."

"I knew I was among microscopic planets!"

"You're among microscopic worlds?!" Braddock stated in complete surprise and amazement.

"Yes, I have two friends right here with me."

"I can't believe this!" Braddock shouted, causing Adrian to flinch from the ear piercing noise.

Braddock's readings picked this up and he made the proper adjustments to the receptive pitch. "Where are you, now?" Braddock questioned after a minute or two.

"I'm with my friends, Rhesus Turnbuckle and Seth Biggs, in a stolen ship called the Van Guard. We are on our way to meet with a king."

"To meet with a king? What for?"

"An evil master called, Diabolis, wants to separate the galaxy Adam and move the various planets to a different point in the solar system."

There came a long eerie pause that gave Adrian a very bad feeling.

"Uh, come back on that?"

"An evil master has a bizarre plan to separate the galaxy Adam."

Braddock took another long pause.

Adrian looked upon the expression of Braddock's intense reflection in his mind's eye and could sense great fear, as Braddock began to analyze with deep sincere thought, his last comment.

"Could you repeat that just one more time," Braddock said, looking painfully at Devon. "Listen to this," he said, handing Devon the earphones.

Adrian's heart began to race. He knew something was terribly wrong. "An evil master has a bizarre plan to separate the galaxy Adam."

Braddock took the headphone back from Devon and stared at his wide open alert eyes. "Are you thinking what I'm thinking?" Braddock questioned.

"Probably, but we can't be sure," Devon responded.

"Did you say that someone is going to separate the atom?"

"Yes."

Braddock dropped the headphones and stared emotionally at Devon again. "Affirmative."

Devon was at a loss for words. "What can we do?" he said, watching Braddock turn and stare at the computer screen.

"What's wrong?" Adrian quizzed, trying to enhance his mind-morphing image of Braddock's face by squinting his eyes.

"Adrian?" Braddock quietly spoke. "The atom is the basic building element of our world. If someone were to split the atom, it would cause an atomic explosion, which could lead to ultimate destruction."

Adrian's face fell white and he leaned back hopelessly in his chair, still eyeing Braddock's face for any sign of a last minute chance at hope. If the separation of planets did in fact mean an atomic explosion for the upper world, it also meant total and complete annihilation of the micro worlds.

"What is it?" Seth asked, adjusting his hat.

Devon interrupted Braddock's thoughts. "Did Adrian say he was going to visit a king?"

"I believe he did," Braddock said. "Adrian, can you hear me?"

"Yeah, I was just telling my friends about our situation. Go ahead."

"Did you say you were going to visit a king?"

"Yes, King Adam. He is the one who named this galaxy after himself."

"Good, I want you to . . ." Braddock's face disappeared and Adrian was once again staring out into space that lay ahead.

"This is bad, huh?" Seth asked.

"This is bad," Adrian confirmed.

"I lost him," Braddock said. "We had a booster failure. I'll have to reboot the system in an hour or so, as soon as she cools off. Looks like we'll have to converse in ten-minute intervals."

"You know, I just realized that he is under the United States Capitol building."

"Oh, no!" Braddock gasped. "The government will think it's a foreign attack! Which means . . ."

"Which means, we'll be in the middle of a world war," Devon said.

"We got to get back on-line and help Adrian get to that king!"

"Or die trying."

7
Diabolic

Diabolis gritted his teeth hard under his tight flesh. "You will suffer no more than this."

"Thank you, sire," the humble Die-cell Captain said gratefully, bowing his head.

"You will die for treason!"

"NO—Please! I beg of you, sire—No . . ."

"Take him away and do with him as you will," Diabolis ordered angrily, his navy blue cape blowing majestically in the gentle Markonia wind. "If anyone of you try to betray me in such a manner as that again, I'll bring an end to this entire regiment! Is that understood?"

"Yes, sire!" the Die-cells snapped in unison, showing no signs of fear.

Diabolis had an old bitter face that was worn down from his evil frown. He had thick white, colorless hair that highlighted his well tanned rustic skin. The only thing left in his cold, lonely heart was that he loved everything about himself and the way things were going in his favor.

He looked over his troops with great admiration and almost brought himself to smile; but he knew that in the hearts of his men, there was no real belief in his cause. Long ago, a commander would never question his motives and would never order him to back down and withdraw a regiment of his finest soldiers so boldly. His men were showing a sign of arrogance more and more, and it was almost a battle to keep the respect of his authority high as well as the duties of ruler and magistrate from being deposed. The mere thought of the physical labor that entails the removal of so many planets, brought the mental capacity of many men crashing to their knees. They did not see this his reign, so close to King Adam, could not exist and have him remain in power. Their retention would be vanquished when his men were promoted to level of incompetence, as sordid as that may sound.

The dawn was breaking and Diabolis would rule all, and for many, a chance of a lifetime was at hand. Of course for many, certain duties were expected to be taken on board—then, at last, Diabolis would be given his due. Meticulous planning and ambitions driven are the only way to true succession! The removal of the kingdom that truly belongs to him must be physically divided and removed to its rightful place in the heavens, however difficult the task.

The planets must be crushed by his military excellence, and the people must learn their place in this new order. Diabolis could just sense the power burning its course through his brain, It was all about 'physical'. In this land where many wanted virtual reality, Diabolis longed to dig his hands in the soil. The very thought of the endless procession of planets moving at his very will, made him hunger for more.

"Sir, we're ready," his trusty Major beckoned.

Diabolis knew the planet Markonia would be the toughest to defeat, because of its strong ties to the Adam Force Alliance. More troops had arrived to help capture the Markonia Empire Building. But Diabolis knew this would not be a job for many, because he had developed a new technology.

The Major put the cacophone loudspeaker to his lips. "This is your last chance! Surrender yourself and your empire, in the name of Diabolis!"

The inner city, surrounded by the huge gray walls, remained silent. There were no windows to be seen, just majestic columns and pillars that appeared an off-green.

The Major looked to Diabolis for approval. Diabolis glared at the city walls and gave a small nod. The Major gave the signal. A huge cumbersome tank, with a long probe extending from the front, slowly rolled to the front gates, making a pleasant crackling sound as it rolled over the loose gravel.

"Radio microwaves ready to activate!" the driver yelled.

"Activate when ready!" the Major called back.

"Yes, sir!"

The people within looked out through small peepholes at the terrifying scene. Their adrenalin began to flow at an uncontrollable rate and their hearts began to beat hard against the inner workings of their chests. They watched as the huge probe from the tank illuminated a bright red strobe that befell the entire Empire Building, causing their hearts to flutter and skip beats. Their legs gave out, and the huge mass of Markonia's finest, collapsed to the floor with uncontrollable spasms.

The hatred that grew in Diabolis's soul pleased him greatly and brought him an overwhelming rush of energy. "That's enough!" he shouted, hating to put an end to the moment.

"Shut her down!" the Major cried to the operator.

The huge tank backed up, turned around, and sped to the huge solid gates. The adjoined ball of solid metal smashed through the gates with ease, and the tank continued in, followed by the anxious troops of soldiers.

Diabolis walked through his new empire's doors and marveled at his new amazing castle. The vast floor reflected the light flickering from the massive chandeliers; the hard soles of his boots clomped and echoed through the corridors, as he proceeded to his new throne room.

Die-cell workers busied themselves removing the old republic rulers, by gagging and tying their hands behind their backs, as they continued to shake with violent convulsions. The radio microwaves only temporarily disabled the old rulers, and when they awoke, they would find themselves in prison camps on Harmoroon-4, a planet farther to the west.

Two Die-cell guards swung the huge doors to the throne room wide open.

Diabolis and his Major marched in gloriously. "This is the moment I've been waiting for my entire life," Diabolis said cunningly, stepping softly on the thick red carpet. Music triumphantly burst forth from the assembled band, presenting a ceremony of sorts. Diabolis reached the steps, proceeded up, turned, and giving a smug wave—sat down comfortably in the astounding throne, declaring himself once and for all—the ruler of Markonia and surrounding commonwealth planets.

The music concluded with one long dashing note, bringing the ceremony to an end. The Major dropped to one knee and bowed humbly before the new ruler. "Sire?" he said, looking up.

"What is it?" Diabolis sneered.

"There is a man here who wishes to speak with you."

"What? Official business already?"

"Do you wish me to send him away?"

"What does he want?"

"He didn't say. He did say his name was Corvolo."

"Ah, yes, Corvolo, an old friend of mine—send him in!"

The guards once again threw the doors open and Corvolo trotted down the red carpet and stopped in front of Diabolis. *"Aroo me sin doust, sire."* (Greetings and hello, sire).

"Waso aheed kin a joust ho?" (What business do you want of me?), Diabolis asked.

"*Mawo mistkin arude meest akin vast Van Guard, tehone aquerst roo jestune vase meenid. Tehone aroost vin alude rewir voust kamo!*" (Three thieves stole a ship I was to sell called the Van Guard; we followed them to this area. We request some of your finest men to join in the search).

"*How dist mistkin vinrogt ships, thronime unst fow!*" (I will lend you two hundred men and fifty five ships, that is all).

"*Vanameere! Vanameere!*" (Thank you, thank you).

Diabolis turned to the Major. "See that this man receives two hundred men and fifty five ships to aid in the search of the thieves."

"Yes, sire!" The Major responded, bowing again.

"*Kist mon geestmine arude restin voe wert asine, how steadern gost amore vin!*" (My comrades believe these thieves are on a personal mission to destroy you, I feel you must come with us).

"*How niemost vern adoe vist, gone sert wost fone!*" (I do not need you to protect me! Be gone, fool!)"

Corvolo bowed. "*De vu minaroon.*" (As you wish). He then turned and left the massive courtroom.

"Prepare a ship! I wish to leave at once!" Diabolis called to the Major.

"But why? We jus arrived here! Don't you wish to stay and enjoy your new kingdom?"

"There will be time for that later. Let us change the orbit of this planet with the Moon Probe, then set a course for Albeta!"

"Sire, the capture of Albeta is not scheduled for another two hundred and fifty hours."

"There has been a sudden change of plans—we will act now! My friend Corvolo would not travel all the way out here, if he did not feel those three thieves were not a true threat."

"But they are mere thieves, sire."

"Never underestimate the power of one man—that can be an entire world's downfall."

"Yes, sire."

Diabolis boarded his small carrier ship and traveled to the nearby moon that cast its image in the distant northern Markonia sky. His ship veered into the moon's long channeled canal, continued until it reached the central docking bay, and came to a silent landing. General Hockingberg approached the ship and stood clear of the lowering hatch. Diabolis emerged from the ship and parted the exhaust that had filled the bay, like a powerful warrior parting the smoke of a freshly fought battle.

"You have arrived early, sire. We were not expecting you so soon," said Die-cell General Hockingberg.

"There has been a change of plans. I wish to change the orbit of Markonia now and begin our capture of Albeta. Now!"

"But, sire, our forces are not yet prepared for . . ."

"I said, now!"

General Hockingberg bowed uneasily. "Yes, sire." He then peered up into Diabolis's face, into the look of dark velocity, into the circle of death that surrounded his being. Diabolis's gaze burned through him, and he ran off to make the necessary arrangements for the planet's removal.

The small moon stopped its rotation and began an unyielding slide in its orbit.

Sand and dirt that had gathered on the moon continued on at speeds over one thousand miles per hour in the moon's intended orbit clockwise around Markonia. The moon shifted smoothly into the ripple of time and space and began to circle Markonia's massive body counterclockwise. Markonia reacted to the moon's new gravitational pull. The huge planet hovered tightly in its loose orbit and was flung like a rock from a slingshot into deep space, as the moon centered itself between Markonia and the sun. The moon followed the racing planet out to space in a swift and turbulent vacuum. The moon countered itself, swinging counterclockwise between Markonia and the deepest reaches of space, bringing the huge planet under control and rolling it to its new orbit among Diabolis's kingdom in the heavens, the small moon only needing to make small corrections in Markonia's course.

Markonia was placed in its rightful orbit near Albeta with practiced ease. Millions upon millions of Die-cell warriors were dispersed from the inner station at the moon's south pole and converged with an unseen wrath of terror upon Albeta's overpopulated cities. The battle raged on for many hours like a constant show of fireworks that could be seen from the moon. Diabolis viewed the show from his deck, as the feeling of triumph filled his pride-filled mind. This was indeed the fulfillment of the true goal that he had envisioned before the downfall of Markonia.

8

The Albeta Warfare Evasion

The Van Guard rocked with a powerful blow. Adrian, Rhesus and Seth grabbed onto anything they could for support.

"What was that?" Seth asked, as the ship settled.

"I think we were hit!" Rhesus said, tightening his grip on the controls.

"Hit? Great, just when things couldn't get any worse," Seth said, looking out among the stars for any signs of movement.

"I don't know, though, this is a new ship, she could be settling," Rhesus questioned.

"Oh, I doubt that!" Seth rebutted.

"So do I!" Rhesus returned.

The ship took another direct hit and rolled over hard and unsteadily among the soft blanket of space.

Seth collected himself and looked over the tracking monitors. "There it is! It's one ship-looks like a Die-cell!"

"Um . . . okay, there should be some rear fighter guns in the stern of the ship!" Rhesus stated, sounding not entirely sure of his new ship.

Adrian knew Rhesus was talking to him. He made his way to the back of the ship and found the oversized guns. He knew he would be of little or no use at shooting down the Die-cell ship because had never been trained to shoot this kind of gun or any kind of gun for that matter. He had never seen or even heard of this kind of gun in his entire short ten years of existence, but as Braddock used to say: "Nothing ventured, nothing gained!"

Whatever that meant. Adrian took his position on the hard metal stool behind the gun, grabbed the handle, and swung the gun to the left, then to the right. This was far easier than he had imagined and was very enjoyable. He looked out at the approaching Die-cell craft that fired a subtle light-blue laser beam that exploded like a stationary bomb fifty feet away. He was suddenly brought back to reality quickly and realized the magnitude of the situation.

"What do you got back there?!" Rhesus yelled.

"One ship! I'll take care of him!" Adrian's eyes scanned the gun quickly for a button or trigger, anything that could fire the gun. He aimed the gun as best he could and squeezed a small trigger that was at hand level. The gun fired a thick bolt of laser energy that exploded under the belly of the Die-cell ship.

"Good shooting!" Rhesus called out.

The Die-cell craft fired again, missing the port side of the Van Guard. Adrian began firing a steady stream of laser power, catching the bridge of the Die-cell craft, sending it into a bright orange fireball. Adrian sat bewildered as Rhesus and Seth cheered.

"That was great!" Seth cried out.

"I didn't think I could hold them off much longer!" Rhesus shouted.

Suddenly the mood changed. "We've got more coming from starboard! Looks like about . . . thirty or so!" Seth cried out.

"Thirty?!"

"Or more! The computer says thirty! I say thirty-five, forty!"

"Biggs, you better get back with Adrian on the guns, I'll try to get us out of here!"

The Die-cell force was upon them in minutes and they could feel the hard pelting of gunfire on the outer hull.

"Our shields are up, but that won't hold them for long!" Rhesus cried out with exaggerated fear. He began to maneuver the ship through the Die-cells like a combat video game, giving Adrian and Seth little time to set up for a shot. They had to fire at random.

Adrian realized that Rhesus and Seth were accomplished warriors, a far cry from the first impression he had of them. He realized now that they had been playing idiots to avoid any confrontation with the commanders from the planet Rolin.

"I'm putting the ship into light-speed! Hold on!" Rhesus quickly made the proper adjustments. The ship jolted, sending and explosion rippling beneath their feet. "I'm not putting the ship into light-speed! They just took it out, and they know it!"

Seth gripped the trigger angrily and panned across the night sky, delivering an onslaught of powerful gunfire, searing the Die-cell ships badly. Adrian glanced over, noticed the beads of sweat streaming down Seth's face and realized the battle was almost over. Everything appeared in slow motion as Rhesus navigated the ship through space with the remaining twenty-five or so Die-cells close behind.

The Die-cells moved to a triangular terrace attack formation to combine their firepower.

"It's over!" Rhesus cried out. "Cease fire!"

"Never!" Seth screamed. "It's never over!"

"It's over! Let's just hope they have mercy on us. Cease fire before you get us all killed—we're no match for them!"

Seth turned loose of his gun and dropped his head in defeat. Adrian gave one last look at the Die-cell formation, staggered his way to the front of the ship, and took his place beside Rhesus. "What do we do now?" he asked softly.

Rhesus didn't answer, he just stared blankly out of the cockpit window. "Biggs, get up here! We've got a problem!"

Seth came running and noticed the problem immediately. The three men stared ahead at an electric sun that produced electric light in many different hues and colors.

"Is that a sun?" Adrian asked.

Seth took his seat next to Adrian. "The computer says it's a planet."

Rhesus gagged on his puzzlement, knowing what system they were in. "Which planet?"

"It says, Albeta."

"That's got to be an electric sun," Rhesus staggered again.

"No, it's Albeta all right . . . in the middle of a world war."

Rhesus eyed the planet closely. The sight seemed almost surreal. "What kind of technology are they using down there?"

Adrian breathed heavily. "I don't know, but I don't like it! Let's get out of here!"

"I think you're right! We'd have a better chance dealing with the Die-cells," Seth stated, attending to the control panel.

"We've definitely got nothing to lose," Rhesus agreed. "But with our hyperdrive out, we won't get to far!"

"Let's go for it!" Adrian shouted.

"Full throttle to port," Rhesus instructed.

"She won't go!" Seth said, struggling again with the controls.

"Try it again!"

"I've tried it twice!"

"Switch to manual!"

Seth made the switch, with the same result. "No good! She won't maneuver! We're being sucked in!"

Rhesus grabbed for the controls, but he felt the uselessness of his actions. The Van Guard smoothly and calmly continued its descent into the atmosphere amid the intense barrage of heavy artillery that engulfed the defenseless ship.

Albeta had a strange attraction that had lured some of the most ruthless and fierce people in the Atom Galaxy to homestead. They built overwhelming cities and constructed a solid line of defense that was unmatched by anything even thought of in the galaxy or neighboring solar systems. Their descendants utilized the power and imagination of their forefathers and had continued to build a secure home for themselves and their posterity. The plan did not call for Diabolis, and the people of Albeta would not stand for his evil ways, even if it meant their lives.

Diabolis knew of this hardy people and knew their capture would be his greatest triumph. He had full knowledge of their fighting potential and dispensed one million Die-cell warriors a day, without fully understanding how the battle below was shaping. His full plan was to saturate the overpopulated planet with nothing but ground troops to prove to the Albetian people his unlimited strength and power, like a delicate artist who proves his worth by showing each brush stroke is a work of art unto itself. Rather than wiping out the entire planet with one blow, he would have something lasting to show for his efforts.

"Switch to auxiliary power!" Rhesus beckoned as a last-ditch effort for their escape.

The radio began to crackle and a harsh, rough sounding voice filled the three men's ears with added fear. "This is Die-cell ship 302! I command you not to flee! Surrender your ship immediately!"

Rhesus switched the radio off. "Increase impulse power!"

Seth made the proper adjustments without contradiction.

"You guys better know what you're doing!" Adrian said.

"We do!" Seth said uneasily, giving a slight unsure glance to Rhesus.

The Van Guard took another unsteady hit.

"They hit us with something that time! They jammed our navigational system! We're not going anywhere they don't want us to go!" Seth said.

Rhesus said nothing and turned the radio back on. "This is Van Guard-one, you got a copy out there?"

"This is Die-cell ship 302! Your ship has been reported stolen, and you have entered restricted property space! You are now under the law of Diabolis, and henceforth all rights and freedoms are revoked! A Die-cell ship will pass and lead you to the Albeta docking bay!"

Rhesus quickly slammed the radio off. His chest burned with anger. He sat back in his seat and let the frustration swell within his mind and soul.

"They're taking us to Albeta?" Adrian asked, knowing it was a stupid question as soon as it left his lips.

"They're going to kill us all! Including themselves!" Rhesus snapped.

A lead Die-cell ship appeared over the top of the Van Guard and headed for the explosive planet that lay ahead. Another shockwave once again stunned and shook the Van Guard from the rear.

"We're going already!" Rhesus shouted to nobody.

Seth steered the Van Guard, tightly following the lead Die-cell craft. Adrian looked out across the approaching Albetian planet. He leaned forward, eagerly fearful, in his seat, and regretfully admired the intense warfare going on below. The night sky filled with the intense light from the massive burnings that illuminated the horrific mushroom clouds scattered throughout multiple continents. Bright sudden lights flashed over the face of the entire planet like flash photography, and three solid red, blue, and green laser beams, equivalent to whole city blocks back home, raced in steady ongoing streams against the planet's orbit which gave the planet the appearance of an electric sun farther out in space.

The Van Guard soon shook with the power of the war raging outside, as the small ship eased its way through the light that reflected on the cockpit window, blinding Seth as he tried to peer at the fading Die-cell craft as it made its way deeper into a thick gray smoke. Rhesus sat up straight in his seat, his anger obviously subsiding, and took control of the ship. Seth sat back in relief, then focused once again on the forsaken terror that surrounded them.

"Why are they taking us to a planet that Diabolis is trying to capture?" Adrian asked.

"In his mind, he's already captured it!" Rhesus quipped.

"There's the landing base ahead!" Seth pointed out.

The Van Guard hovered momentarily, then settled to the ground. The outer hatch pelted by intense gunfire, blew wide open, admitting fifteen or so Die-cell soldiers with guns pointed. "Put your hands behind your head!" one shouted, behind his thick rubber mask.

The three men cooperated. They faced the Die-cell soldiers, stood, placed their hands behind their heads, and slowly walked to the hatch where they saw another fifty soldiers that had surrounded the ship.

"Shouldn't you guys be fighting a battle?!" Rhesus said, waiting for a response. He suddenly jerked, as a quick, sharp, deep pain shot up the back of his right leg. He took advantage of the moment and staggered into one of the unsuspecting Dei-cell men, knocking him to the ground.

Adrian and Seth rushed to his aid.

"Freeze! Back up!" came another muffled voice.

The Die-cells snatched Rhesus from the ground and carried him off, then motioned for Seth and Adrian to follow. They quickly placed their hands once again behind their heads and followed the trail Rhesus's boots made in the dirt, as the fierce Die-cells dragged him along painfully.

Adrian suddenly caught a glimpse of something dashing across the sky, through the drifted smoke. "Did you see that?" he quietly asked Seth.

"See What?"

"It looked as if . . . as if the moon just raced across the sky."

"No moon can race that fast."

Adrian curiously returned his gaze upward as the moon rolled its way across the sky as it had done before. He turned to the guard walking alongside of him. "Can I ask you a question?" he said.

"What?" the soldier demanded angrily.

"This is a terrific planet your force has decided to capture!"

"Yeah, so what's your question?"

"Can you explain the moon?"

"It's no moon. It's a space probe used to circle the planet against the orbit and relocate it to its new kingdom."

Adrian looked into his face. "So, that's how you're separating the atom!"

The soldier returned the stare. "Right, I . . ." He suddenly grasped his chest and fell dead. The soldier behind advanced stepping on the dead man without a flinch. "You talk too much," he mumbled.

Adrian quickly turned his solemn glare to the ground and continued his quick pace behind Rhesus. The small troop came upon the Die-cell commander and inquired what to do. The shadowy figure gave a quick sentence of death, nodded, then disappeared. They unhesitatingly threw Rhesus into a nearby wall, followed by Seth. Adrian knew it was over. He gasped what would be his final deep breath and trundled forward to the thick, brown, rock wall. He would not face the Die-cells; they would have to shoot him in the back. Rhesus and Seth gazed at him in lost friendship and faced the wall as well. They could hear the Die-cells behind preparing to fire. Adrian only prayed this end would lead to his passage back to Braddock and the life that he had built and left behind.

The wall suddenly began to shake. A fountain of men poured over the top like water boiling over. They screamed their blood-curdling war cry and crushed the Die-cells beneath them like bugs. The Die-cell soldiers tried to fire their weapons, but it was too late, they had no warning. The Die-cells that did survive ran off into the battle that raged on around them, chased by half the contradicting warriors.

"Are you guys all right?!" the squad leader asked.

"We're fine, but how do we get off this rock?" Rhesus said.

The squad leader chuckled. "You must have been a passerby when your ship was captured."

"That's right; our ship is back at the docking bay," Adrian said.

"So, you don't mind if we use it?" the squad leader said, keeping his eyes open for any Die-cells.

"What for?" Seth questioned.

"We're on a reconnaissance mission! We believe Diabolis's next move with the Moon Probe will be the smaller planet Gyrone. We need to get to it before he does."

"Why don't you use your own ships?" Rhesus said, impatiently.

"The Die-cells knocked out our entire fleet two days ago. We now have to scrounge for anything we can get, like personal ships, hover crafts, anything!"

"Well, you're not just going to leave us here!" Rhesus demanded.

"No, you'll be coming with us! How many people can your ship hold?"

At the most, maybe ten people."

"That will have to do! You said your ship was at the docking bay?"

Seth hesitated, "What if we don't want to do the mission?"

"Then you are stuck here!" the squad leader said, running off.

The three men looked at each other disconcertingly, then followed.

Adrian lost sight of the squad leader momentarily. "Where did he go?!"

"Over there!" Seth said, pointing to the north.

Rhesus, Seth, and Adrian came up behind the squad leader who was sprawled out on the ground on a short high-rise overlooking the docking bay. "Is that your ship down there?" he asked, gripping his gun tightly.

"Yes, sir," Adrian responded.

"Ah, a Van Guard! How did three guys like you afford a Van Guard?"

"Uh, inheritance," Rhesus lied.

"Not bad!" the squad leader said, nodding to the rest of his squad, who were impressed as well. "Looks like it's being guarded by about fifteen—maybe twenty men!" he continued.

"Did you have any idea how we can get to the ship?" Adrian asked.

The leader paused. "Does your ship have a shield?"

"Of course!" Rhesus confided.

The leader pointed to Seth and Adrian, "You and you, go down there an create a disturbance!" He then motioned to Rhesus. "While they are keeping the Die-cells busy, you get on the ship and activate the shield!"

"Yes, sir," Rhesus responded with a loose salute.

"Waite a minute!" Seth interrupted, pushing his hat back. "How are we going to create a disturbance?"

"Easy! You are now officially Die-cell soldiers!"

A trooper approached, opened his pack, and pulled out two Die-cell uniforms. He handed one to Adrian and one to Seth, then reformed rank without saying a word.

"The rest is up to you!" the leader stated with a smile. He turned his attention to the rest of his squad. "Secure the premises! We don't want our comrades thinking our friends here are real Die-cells!"

"Yes, sir!" they called back, running through the smoke in formation.

The leader turned to Rhesus. "Here's a comlink, notify me the minute the shield has been activated—but whatever you do, stay on the ship and make sure the hatch is sealed securely!"

"Yes, sir!" Rhesus said again, taking the comlink.

"Are you guys ready?" the leader continued.

"As ready as we'll ever be!" Adrian said.

Moments passed and Seth and Adrian stood nervously before the small Die-cell unit, dressed in their mock uniforms. They could sense this stunt would never work, as the Die-cells eyed them over suspiciously.

"What do we do now?" Adrian uttered under his breath.

Seth turned and looked at Adrian. "Let's argue—maybe we can start a brawl."

"I refuse, sir!" Adrian shouted, disguising his ambiguous tones.

"How dare you refuse a senior officer!"

"How come you get to play the senior officer," Adrian complained silently.

"Because, I look more like a senior officer," Seth mumbled in return.

"You look nothing like a senior officer!" Adrian bellowed.

"I do so! You are cut from rank, solider!"

"You can't do that! You have no authority!" Adrian yelled, pushing Seth backwards.

The Die-cell guards approached slowly, forming a semi-circle. Rhesus saw his chance. He noticed that the hatch to the ship had been lowered; he could only hope that no Die-cells were aboard. He embraced his gun in one hand and comlink in the other, like a last minute check—then made his move. He ran hard, across the rough cement landing pad, and bounded up into the ship. The ship was empty. If there had been any Die-cell soldiers, Seth and Adrian had managed to pull them out. Rhesus paused, backed himself against the wall, and looped his finger over the trigger of his gun—in the event they had seen him and were making their way back to the ship.

Rhesus listened intently, as Seth and Adrian continued to quarrel outside. He quickly peeked out through the open hatch and noticed they had not witnessed his stunt. He took a deep relaxing breath and manned to the controls, closing the hatch abruptly.

The Die-cells turned, aiming their guns. Seth had to do something; he hauled back and swung his fist across Adrian's cheek. Adrian collapsed to the ground. It worked! The Die-cells returned their full attention back to the fight to watch Adrian retaliate.

Rhesus switched the meter to 1-4-5, until it had a reading of 9-847. "The shield is now functional! The shield is now functional!" he recited into the comlink,

Seth stumbled backward, trying to keep his balance. Adrian leapt through the air with a flying tackle, sending the two men skidding across the rough landing pad. They could hear the reaction of the Die-cells reacting with a repulsive moan. Seth threw another punch with his wounded arm, rendering Adrian unconscious. The Die-cell soldiers cheered uncontrollably, waving their guns in the air. Seth sat up trying to focus his eyes and looked at Adrian lying on his back in a deep sleep. Out of the corner of his eye, he noticed the green flag wave briskly through the air once. He knew that was the sign from the squad leader for them to evacuate. He tried in desperation to wake his friend up. "Adrian, come on! Get up!" Seth cried. He could tell that the Die-cells were growing suspicious. Without much effort he grabbed Adrian by the ankles and dragged him across the landing pad, with his head bouncing along behind over the rough terrain.

The Die-cells stood motionless, not knowing whether to follow or stay and guard the ship. Seth pulled Adrian into the deep, rich, thick ivleen bushes that grew along side the tarmac. He glanced back, pushed his helmet back from his eyes, and watched the Die-cell soldiers as the squad leader ordered the drop of the Wy-ok missile.

The red, blue, and green thick laser lights high in the sky, which the threesome had seen circling the planet from space, made another pass. The

Wy-ok missile, a massive ball of pure invisible energy, fell silently from its source around the red laser stream.

The energy Wy-ok missile fell harshly upon the Van Guard, leaving nothing but a thick cloud of dust in its wake. Seth bit his lip and looked Adrian over again for any change in his condition. Nothing. The cloud of dust calmly settled gently into the subtle wind, contrary to the brutal war.

Alone sat the Van Guard in a giant crater of dust among the song of war. The Die-cell guards were nowhere to be seen.

"Quite a shield you got on that Van Guard!" the squad leader shouted, running toward the ship.

Seth grabbed Adrian and slid him gently down the side of the crater. Six other squad troopers aided him by carrying Adrian up into the hatch of the Van Guard without hesitation.

The craft fired up its boosters, hovered, then sped from the atmosphere. Next stop, Gyrone!

9

The Moon Probe

Adrian awoke and quietly eyed the crew of the ship, wondering about each and the lives they had led. Suddenly, something jolted deep within him, something deep within his soul. He looked around and noticed everyone else had experienced the same shock wave. He grasped the arm of his chair tightly and began to mentally beg for the feeling to subside.

The squad leader fell from his seat, followed by a number of his troopers.

The feeling lifted into oblivion as quickly as it had settled.

"What was that?" Seth asked.

"It has reached the halfway mark," Adrian remarked.

The squad leader arose from the floor and turned to Adrian in a military step. "What has reached its halfway mark?" he inquired.

"The splicing of the atom, it's halfway over," Adrian said, seeping through his daze.

"That must have been the vacuum that we felt from the separation!" Seth said.

"Yes!" Adrian replied, "I'm almost sure of it!"

"I demand to know what you are talking about!" the leader shouted.

Rhesus held the controls of the craft tightly and stared straight ahead. "According to Adrian, Diabolis's separation of the planets will divide something called an 'atom', which is the smallest unit that makes up larger worlds—that's where Adrian comes from!"

"We must stop Diabolis, and I must find a way home!" Adrian said.

"That's ludicrous!" the leader scoffed.

"I believe him!" Rhesus confided.

"That's all well and good," the leader continued. "But we are on our way to stop Diabolis!"

Rhesus paused. "That's not good enough! We need to cancel the mission and proceed to find King Adam."

The squad leader flew across the floor of the ship and peered face to face with Rhesus, his hot breath beating down against his cheek. "Where is your king! Your king has forsaken you! We now must find a way to conquer Diabolis on our own!"

Rhesus held his ground. "That's not a good idea! One planet of savage warriors is not enough to conquer the combined power of Diabolis! We must do it right by asking a higher power. As soon as King Adam sees his people come together and show that they really care, he will crush Diabolis and his forces. Again, I must insist we change present course and proceed to King Adam and return to the eastern Atom Galaxy!"

Seth checked his navigational readings. "It's too late; we're coming upon Gyrone, now!"

"Good!" the leader said, correcting his posture. "If I am correct, the Moon Probe should appear at oh-one-hundred, which would make it right about, now!"

Seth poured over his readouts on the computer screen again, then looked painfully at Rhesus. "He's right! The Moon Probe is arriving from the rear at one-thousand kilometers; in five minutes we'll be on their scanners."

The squad leader once again turned to Rhesus. "If we wait for your precious king, all the people on Gyrone will be wiped out, and you will be held responsible!"

Rhesus said nothing.

"We have an entire fleet arriving from ships gathered from neighboring planets around Albeta! I say we strike now!"

A small red light on the control board began to flicker in sequence.

"We're receiving a light-bead code!" Seth advised.

The leader translated the message. "It reports Albeta has been captured!" he said, turning back to Rhesus. "Do you have a better resolution?"

Rhesus kept his gaze straight ahead toward the planet Gyrone. "I guess we have no choice."

"Good boy!" the leader acknowledged. "We will reside on the dark side of the planet until the moon appears in the sky. My orders were that the main force will form a barrier around the outer moon, trapping it between themselves and Gyrone. We will wait for a further squad of ships, approach the moon's surface, and search for it's weakness! Is that understood?"

"It will never work!" Rhesus stated.

"What makes you so sure?"

"Because the Moon Probe was designed to move planets; surely it can shake off a few pathetic ships!"

The massive, rough face of the Moon Probe rolled it's way into view. "We are out of coordinates!" the leader shouted, ignoring Rhesus's advice. "Cut to hyper-drive, now!" he ordered.

"I'm sorry," Seth stammered, "its speed didn't coincide with my readings—it must have scrambled our signals!"

"Hyper-drive, now!" the leader repeated.

"Look!" a trooper shouted.

Through the clouds of Gyrone, out over the horizon, appeared a large squadron of various ships of all shapes and sizes that flew together in attack formation. The lead ship fired up his rockets, followed by the others in a domino effect, and rocketed toward the moon's surface.

"They're attacking!" the leader yelled. "Your instruments are wrong! We should have arrived earlier!"

"They scrambled our signals!" Seth declared again.

"I ordered hyper-drive! But change coordinates to the moon's surface!"

"Don't do it, Biggs!" Rhesus pleaded.

"Do it! Or I'll execute you myself!" the leader said, pressing a gun to the back of Seth's head.

"I have no choice!"

"We are going in blind! We have no attack plan!"

"I repeat, set coordinates to moon's surface!"

Seth hesitantly began to change the navigational course. The deep rumble poured from the boosters, and the small ship plummeted towards the moon's rough exterior.

"We're coming in too fast! Slow her down!" the leader ordered.

"I can't!" Seth shouted, trying in desperation to steer the ship away.

Rhesus grabbed the controls. "It's no use!" he cried.

The huge crater before them twisted open, revealing a giant gaping cave. Rhesus loosened his grip on the controls. "They used our advance to cover their tracting beam," he said, turning loose of the controls altogether.

The Van Guard continued slowly into the deep, pitch-black bowels of the moon. The boosters roared, echoing through the darkness, and bouncing off the hidden walls. The blue-and-orange flames continued to erupt from the ship's large rockets, pushing hard against an unseen force that demanded they hover slowly onward to unseen danger.

"Shut the rockets off! They aren't doing us any good!" Rhesus said to Seth, eyeing the squad leader in disgust.

The squad leader said nothing.

"Do we have any lights so we can see?" Adrian asked.

"Activating flood lights," Seth responded.

The lights flickered on and radiated toward the walls. Everyone peered forward, trying to catch a glimpse of the cave's interior. The light delivered a steady stream that disappeared into the black abyss, finding no reflection of the rocky wall, only a thin stream of fog that drifted into the light.

"Nothing!" Seth mentioned.

"It's just too dark!" Rhesus stated.

The Van Guard suddenly quickened its pace and was escorted into a large, multi-level, well-lit docking area. The small crew looked on in horror, as they beheld the sight of more that a million armed Die-cell soldiers awaiting their arrival. An enormous metallic door silently slid shut behind them, securing their fate.

"Where are the other ships?" Adrian asked.

"Who knows? Maybe down other shafts or hurtling through space like lost insects." Rhesus conceded.

The small party soon found themselves standing precariously outside the ship, restrained in tight-fitting laser cuffs and begging for mercy from the Die-cell Moon Probe commander. His very presence was hard and cold; he slowly moved forward, instigating great fear in Adrian and the others.

"Take these men to the rear holding cells!" he commanded, calmly placing his hands on his hips. "Let them sit for a while, then record their names and issue them with identification codes! What you do with them after that is up to you! Have fun with them-and make an example out of them!"

Adrian's heart beat wildly against his chest as the guards led them down the long corridors. The walls appeared white and clean, contrary to a dark force such as the Die-cells. They ushered the men into large gray circular holding cells and activated the invisible force field. Adrian's mind continued to race with turmoil; he thought back to Braddock and his home that was so close, yet so far away, and wondered if he would ever return. He sat down on the cold impersonal floor and began to wait his destiny.

"We can't let them do this to us!" Rhesus complained, tugging on the laser cuffs the Die-cells had left on.

"Do you have any suggestions?" Seth inquired.

"No way we're going to get out of this one, not in the center of a giant moon such as this!" the leader commented.

"I wonder whose fault this is?" Rhesus said, glaring at the leader.

"You can't talk to a senior officer that way!" the leader shouted.

"No, but I can talk to a fellow prisoner any way I want to!"

"Why, you little, cheesy lummox!" The leader lunged forward and wrapped his laser cuffs around Rhesus's throat, choking him.

Seth and the troopers jumped to his rescue, throwing each one to different sides of the room.

"Calm down, now! We have to work together or we will never get out alive!" Seth bellowed.

"I think that decision has already been made!" Rhesus argued.

"There's still hope—there's always hope! But we have to work together to develop a plan of action!"

"I wonder what they'll do to us?" one of the troopers calmly said.

"I don't know," Seth confided

"I'll tell you what will happen! We will definitely . . ." Adrian tuned everything out as the image of Braddock appeared once again before him.

"Can you read me?" Braddock asked, giving Adrian a comforting smile.

"Loud and clear!" Adrian responded.

Rhesus, Seth, and the others turned and stared at Adrian curiously.

"He must be picking up his friend, Braddock! They can communicate by some means!" Seth said, kneeling next to Adrian.

"Sorry I cut you off last time; we had a booster failure! How are things going?" Braddock said, with unquestionable charm.

"The separation of the Atom Galaxy is half complete. I could feel it; there is a giant suction forming from the removal of the planets. And worse yet, we are being held captive in the middle of the Moon Probe, in some kind of holding cell behind a clear force field."

"Hey, you!" a voice interrupted.

Seth glanced up and noticed a single Die-cell soldier standing on the other side of the force field.

"Yeah?" Seth responded.

"You guys got half a naroon left, then you will be disposed of!" he uttered scornfully.

"On behalf of the Atom Force! I demand you let us go!" the leader demanded, trying to intimidate the guard through the thick shield.

The guard began to laugh uncontrollably. "I take great pleasure in my work!" Then he disappeared.

Adrian returned his attention back to Braddock's face. "Sorry about that interruption," he said, trying to hold back his fear of death.

"That's all right!" Braddock said, taking a long pause. "I heard your friends talking in the background! Was their voice carrying through the force field?"

"Yes."

"That's what I thought!" He took another long pause. "I think I just thought of a way for you to escape the force field!"

"You did?"

"I find it very fascinating that a human cannot penetrate a force field, but the human voice can. The voice is just as real in substance as your fingers or your hand, considering you are a replicated aura. Adrian, when you first appeared to myself and Devon, my hand went right through you! Do you still have that capability?"

"I . . . I don't know? I've never used it!"

"You've got to try! You've got to do it!"

"I don't know if I can!"

"You've got to believe in yourself. I do!"

Adrian smiled and held his hands and the laser cuffs out in front of him. His mind ran through every emotion he could think of, joy, rapture, sadness, pain, humility, and anger. Adrian fell backward, landing painfully on his back, and stared up at the ceiling. "I can't do it!"

"Yes, you can!" Braddock shouted. "What went through your mind when I grabbed you ten years ago?!"

Adrian sat upright again. "I . . . I . . ." He paused. "I saw a giant fingerprint! A big green fingerprint!"

"Well then, picture in your mind, a big green fingerprint!"

Adrian set the image in his mind. The fingerprint began to swirl ferociously, then stopped as fast as it had begun. Adrian slowly opened his eyes and noticed the laser cuffs had fallen to the floor, "It worked!"

"I knew it would! Now, let's get you and your friends out of there!"

Adrian stood and approached the force field. It rippled before him, appearing like a soft fragile clear liquid.

"Adrian, you can do it." Rhesus cautioned.

Adrian placed his hands in front of him again; his fingers hovering barely above the certain death that would surely ensue. He glanced up to Braddock's face that gave him a confident smile, then disappeared. Adrian closed his eyes and watched the fingerprint dance rhythmically in his mind's eye. He fell forward and tumbled to the floor. His eyes flew open, and he turned to see his friends on the other side of the force field.

Rhesus was stunned. He quickly approached the shield and gave Adrian the necessary directions to shut the field down. The force field fell from sight with a crackling zip. Rhesus and the others emerged cautiously from their cell and silently looked around for any Die-cell guards.

"What about our laser cuffs?" Seth asked.

"I'll have to re-circuit the force field controls!" the leader said, opening the control box.

"What does that have to do with anything," Seth asked.

"If I can reactivate half of the shield, we can snap the cuffs off in a heartbeat!"

"Yeah, good idea! But hurry!"

The computer began to crackle with an electronic hiss. "Please enter access code," it replied.

"I'll have to override the system!" the leader stated.

"Hurry! The guards are probably tracking our movements right now!" Seth said, as panic began to set in.

"Ha! I got it!" the leader cheered, watching half the force field reform in its original shape. He slid his cuffs down the long edge with sparks flying across the corridor. He turned his head away as his cuffs flew off. "Follow me!" he cried, dashing down the long hallway.

"No! You'll . . ." Rhesus cried.

The lights suddenly dimmed to an eerie pulsating red.

". . . set off the motion detectors!" Rhesus continued.

The squad troopers quickly snapped off their cuffs and followed their leader. Rhesus watched as the troop disappeared from sight. "Looks like were on our own!" he said.

Adrian, Rhesus, and Seth Biggs slid their cuffs along the rough edge of the shield, cutting themselves loose, then hastily ran down the corridor in the opposite direction with Adrian close behind.

They bounded around a sharp corner and stopped short. "It's a dead end!" Adrian panicked.

"Dead is right!" Seth answered.

The red haunting light continued to fill the Moon Probe's passages and channels. "We have an escape in cell block 542! We have an escape in cell block 542! All hands to 542! I repeat, all hands to 542! A voice called out over the intercom.

Seth gasped as the Die-cells poured down the corridor armed and ready to kill. "Do something!" he pleaded.

Rhesus stared at the ceiling; maybe there was a way to cut through it and climb through a shaft. Adrian began banging on the thick wall and crying out for Braddock to return.

The wall suddenly slid open, revealing a thick stone closet.

"What did you do?" Rhesus said.

"I don't know!" Adrian responded.

The three men raced inside and slid the door closed behind them. The Die-cells turned the corner and began to ferociously beat the door down. The noise echoed through the small stone room, imploring the three men to try harder at their escape. Adrian ran his fingers along each stone, praying for another miracle.

10

Anti-Orbit Gears

"They're ramming the door!" Seth cried hysterically.

The huge ram crashed through the large door, ripping it like paper. The Die-cells abruptly pushed forward and crumbled what was left of the door to the ground.

Adrian jumped to his feet and pressed his back as far to the wall as it would go.

"Fire!" the Die-cell commander ordered, his voice flooding Adrian's ears. "FIRE!"

The ground twitched beneath Adrian's feet and the room took off horizontally away from the Die-cells, leaving them stunned. The room sped to a screeching halt and then dropped straight down. Adrian hovered briefly and then dropped to the floor, as the room stopped once again. The sound of scrapping metal slowly filled the small stone chamber, as the room slowly began to tilt forward. Seth toppled over, landed on Adrian's head, and continued on over the open edge where the Die-cells had once stood. Adrian skidded his heels back, clamoring desperately for the far wall, away from the darkness that lay below. Rhesus screamed in terror as he too plunged over the edge.

Adrian flung his arms in every direction, searching for something to grasp. Anything. The room tilted straight down, and he slid uncontrollably into the unknown. He soon landed harshly in a similar room of stone, jarring his left knee. He sat up and noticed Seth and Rhesus standing and admiring the small environment.

"This looks familiar!" Rhesus said.

Adrian looked around and noticed the room was the same as the one they had just fallen from. He felt the floor twitch beneath his feet as he had before; he held his breath and prepared for another fall. The wall from behind the three men slid open, revealing another similar room.

"What is this?" Adrian questioned.

"I don't know!" Seth answered, pushing his hat back out of his eyes.

They hesitantly entered the other room, and the wall from the opposite side fired open, revealing yet another tiny room of stone.

"This is . . . almost like a maze!" Seth pointed out, following Rhesus into the small enclosure.

The wall closed tightly behind the three men. Adrian was beginning to feel claustrophobic; he sat down in the middle of the floor quietly and awaited any more doors to open. The room jolted and slowly rolled horizontally again. It felt to Adrian like a train ride he had taken with Braddock five years ago. It was very relaxing.

Seth and Rhesus sat down next to Adrian and were beginning to enjoy the ride. "I don't think this is a maze . . . but I might know what it is!" Rhesus murmured.

"What?" Adrian asked inquisitively.

"Well," Rhesus said, pausing. "I'm not sure, but I believe these small rooms are the Moon Probe's anti-orbit gears!"

"What is that supposed to mean?" Seth asked.

"We are probably in, or near the center of the Moon Probe. It probably uses these small stone rooms as weights, in a way, to counterbalance the moon's orbit—steering it in the direction!"

"I get it!" Adrian said. "These hollow stone blocks will all move to one side, forcing the moon to roll against its orbit!"

"That's right, more or less."

Th stone confinement rolled to a stop and the three friends continued, making their way down various passages of interlocking large stone capsules.

They stopped.

"This has got to be the center of the Moon Probe!" Rhesus commented.

The three men looked out over a massive body of water that rocked a single, thundering wave back and then forth in a steady calming motion. Billions of stone chambers surrounded the water on all sides and arched high overhead. The sight made Adrian quiver. The stone workings pivoted, rotated, and slid with precision to interlock with other columns.

"They look like they're alive," Adrian said, mesmerized.

"They do," Rhesus quipped, seeming not to care.

"It appears their movement is computer controlled! It's amazing how anybody can cheat space and time in this manner!" Seth said, his hat falling into his eyes.

"The laws of space and time are pretty simple, once you figure out all the answers—and that's the hard part!" Rhesus exclaimed. "But now back to reality! How are we going to get across this thing?"

"What makes you think we want to go across?" Seth asked, "I'd rather go up!"

"Up?"

"I agree with Seth," Adrian responded. "That water looks too dangerous!"

Rhesus knew he was outnumbered and quickly gave in. "All right, but there's really no telling where we'll end up."

"Whichever way we go!" Adrian added.

The three men scanned the walls of the stone superstructure for an upward transport and ducked inside the next one that came along.

"This thing is so efficient, it doesn't waste power by making noise!" Rhesus pointed out.

Adrian nodded in agreement, but something suddenly seemed wrong. Something with the ride twisted his emotions differently than he had felt before. His suspicions were confirmed when the room rotated and threw Seth far out into the air over the giant wave that roared below. He couldn't believe what he was seeing, Seth vibrant and alive one minute, then his life ebbing away the next.

Seth catapulted through the thick, rich air that wafted up from the wave. The rush of the wind seemed to grab his soul and expand his inner fear, ringing it out like a thick liquid from a cloth. He hung on to his hat and screamed.

Rhesus had no time to think; he backed up and then bolted into the air, following his friend Seth. Adrian watched as the two disappeared beneath the murky blue-gray waters, not to come up again.

Adrian jumped to the next stone transport going down, ran to the water's edge, and eyed the wave desperately. Twenty feet out Seth's hat floated solemnly on the smaller waves washing to shore. He jumped in, grabbed it, and waded slowly back to the rocky beach.

Rhesus splashed into the freezing, rushing water after Seth and grabbed hold of him around his chest. Seth's lungs quickly filled with water, and he passed out coldly in Rhesus's arms.

"Biggs!" Rhesus yelled, losing the feeling in his own legs. "Wake up!"

The water suddenly befell the color of shadow.

Rhesus glared upward at the enormous wall of water that soon arrived. He closed his eyes tightly and prepared for the worst. Seth snapped free from Rhesus's arms and was swiftly carried upward into the sky by the great wave. Rhesus soon followed.

Adrian continued to search and scan the mountain of water, as well as the distant shore for his friends. Suddenly, something caught his eye! He noticed a small point of color amid the top of the wave—that must be them!

Rhesus saw the moving stone walls closing in rapidly as the wave carried them faster to certain death and threatened to smash them into the wall like bugs. He swam back as hard as he could to avoid decapitation if the wave should crash too hard. He and Seth sailed into an open room and were almost washed back out again. Rhesus's fingers grabbed the stone ledge and he held on for dear life, with Seth dangling dangerously below. Every muscle in his face strained painfully as he tried in desperation to pull the two of them to safety. His teeth began to grind; his fingers began slipping on the wet stone; his arms aching with the added weight. He moaned a deep, painful howl, as he swung his friend into the room.

Adrian frantically ran for the moving wall and leapt inside. He dashed artfully from room to room, upwards to his awaiting friends.

Rhesus gave one final shove to his friend Seth, pushing him farther into the room. Knowing his best friend was safe from harm, it was time for him to go—he closed his eyes and relaxed his tight, painful grip from the sharp stone. He was now free. It was over.

Rhesus jerked to a halt in mid-air, as some force wrapped around his wrist, knocking his elbow and shoulder out of socket. He quickly opened his eyes and looked up into a familiar face. "Adrian!" he cried in delight.

"You don't think I'd let you go that easily, do you?" Adrian said, pulling Rhesus to steady ground, the water washing over their feet from another wave. Rhesus tripped, catching himself on the support of Adrian's shoulder, "Steady!" Adrian cautioned, sitting Rhesus on the floor against the cold, hard, stone wall.

"Is Biggs all right?" Rhesus asked, rubbing his arm.

"Yeah, just fine! Only a little water in his lungs!"

Seth crawled into Rhesus's view and sat next to him. "Are *you* all right?"

"Yeah . . . it's just . . . I don't know where to go from here." Rhesus stammered.

The wall from behind began to roll open. Rhesus and Seth backed away and awkwardly stumbled to their feet.

"Looks like we'll just keep finding our way through the passages!" Adrian chimed in. But this room was different; the feeling he had felt just before

Seth had fallen, suddenly deepened. The room emitted a strange bright light that floated around on an ocean of terror.

"I don't know about this?" Seth shyly uttered.

"You feel it too?" Adrian asked, not expecting an answer.

The room, complete with smooth, dull gray walls, was quite large. It took the appearance of some type of control room, but no instruments, furniture, windows, or anything that possibly reflected any personality could be seen. Rhesus cautiously looked around the room and ushered himself in.

"I'm not going in there!" Seth said, biting his lip nervously.

Adrian said nothing and quickly followed Rhesus, leaving Seth shaking with fear behind. Rhesus stopped crisply in the middle of the room, not taking his eyes off the walls, as Adrian and Seth came up and stopped behind him. "This is odd!" he said.

"I don't find it odd at all!" A deep resonating voice echoed from all around. "In fact, I call it my quarters."

Rhesus, Adrian, and Seth froze and remained motionless, their hearts pounding wildly. The room suddenly became festooned with bizarre framed art and some furniture.

"Now, may I ask why you intrude?"

The three men turned to see a man standing stationary, dressed head to toe in a leather suit of mail. They could feel the circle of death that surrounded him casting its brutal image into their consciousness.

"I said, why do you fools intrude?!" he yelled vehemently, his voice cutting through them like sharp knives.

Rhesus looked deep into the man's face, braving his inner horror. "I know you . . ." he gasped.

The man's gaze burned through Rhesus with a murderous tendency of homicidal abhorrence. The room suddenly grew darker; the air grew colder, as a thick wind circled the three men with an onslaught of dark velocity.

"You . . . you're Diabolis!" Rhesus's voice trembled with anguish.

The man hesitated and smiled, sensing Rhesus's fear. "Yes," he said, approaching the terrified crew.

Rhesus held his ground; he had been waiting for this moment for a very long time. "My name is Rhesus, and I have come to destroy you!" he said sternly, in a confidant practiced voice.

Diabolis stopped his advance and placed his index finger dramatically to his lips. "You must be the three petty thieves. Corvolo was right—he must have seen something in you that I can't. I don't know how you arrived, but today is the day you will die!" he said, rushing toward Rhesus.

Rhesus pulled a small hidden gun from his belt and fired six rounds in quick succession.

Diabolis was unfazed and advanced faster. "This is my domain, I am untouchable!" he cried, pulling out an electrical rod and striking Rhesus in the belly with a powerful electrical bolt. He laughed his grinding laugh and swung around, catching Seth across his chest, sending him tumbling backward.

Rhesus stooped over in pain, staying strong to his feet. Diabolis would not win, not this time! His reign of terror would come to an end. Now! Forgetting about his wounds, he clutched his gut tightly and reaching down deep into the very fiber of his being, he roared with everything he had left, his maddening war cry! His legs trembled unsteadily far below his anger-filled head; but he pressed on, sure of Diabolis's doom.

Diabolis backed up, not sure what to make of the situation. He calmly looked down, pulled out his gun from its black holster, and pointed it directly between Rhesus's eyes. Rhesus ignored the gun and continued his set path to Diabolis. Diabolis gently squeezed the trigger; a dark purple laser bolt ricocheted from the chamber and knocked Rhesus to the ground in painful agony.

Adrian was helpless. He watched Rhesus fall with the loud pop and sparks that flew from the laser beam upon impact. Diabolis turned and stared toward him; he panicked! He closed his eyes tightly and pictured the large green fingerprint.

"I need Die-cell reinforcements to my quarters!" Diabolis spouted off into thin air.

"Yes, sir, right away!" a voice responded.

Adrian could feel the floor beneath him slide up his legs as he melted through it, but he dared not open his eyes. On the floor below, an unsuspecting woman typed diligently away at her computer; something moved quickly in the corner of her eyes. She glanced up and noticed Adrian's legs dangling from the ceiling. Impulse raced through her brain; she kicked her chair back and bolted to the water cooler, screaming. Her colleagues rushed in to her aid and gasped at the ghostly sight.

Adrian stagnantly hovered downward through the computer and on through to the next floor. The superior grabbed desperately at him but felt nothing.

"This place is haunted! I quit!" she shouted, storming out.

11

Galla

Adrian drifted down through the Moon Probe's interior and phased himself out through the moon's thick crust. He continued down through space itself and gallantly landed softly on the surface of the planet Galla, Diabolis's most recent capture.

Adrian stared at the darkness behind his eyelids and cautiously opened his eyes to the new planet. It was rich with vegetation and brightly colored foliage that covered gently rolling hills as far as the eye could see. Around the perimeter grew a thick mass of trees that provided the beautiful setting with a comfortable shade. The atmosphere filled his mind with pleasant thoughts that almost erased the memory of his lost friends. He settled down upon the thick green grass and rested his aching back into the nook of a giant rock that held fast and secure to the very depths of this strange new planet.

Adrian listened and felt the wind as it rustled through the leaves high over head. His stomach sank. All the memories of what had happened to his friend's minutes ago suddenly came flooding back like a giant tidal wave. The tears swelled behind his eyes; he clenched his eyes tightly closed, trying to regain control.

The blurry image of Braddock slowly appeared, easing some of the tension. Adrian broke down. "I killed them! I killed my friends!" he cried, covering his face in shame.

"Calm down, calm down. What happened?" Braddock asked, in his reassuring tone.

"I ran! I ran when they needed me the most!" He looked up into Braddock's face and explained the explicit details of his friend's capture and downfall. "I wish to return to our world! Iit's time for me to come home!"

The image of Braddock's face froze in mid-air.

Braddock paused the transmission and turned to Devon. "He wishes to return home, but I don't have the capabilities."

Devon took a seat in a nearby chair and pondered the situation over quickly. "I really believe he should stay!" he said.

"Why?" Braddock asked, confused.

"He needs to complete the mission for his friends' sake."

Braddock turned away in sorrow; he knew Devon was right. But how much longer until he could see Adrian again; how much longer would this mission even last—or would he ever see Adrian again?! He reconnected the transmission and released the pause. "Adrian?" he uttered.

"Yes."

"We think it's best if you complete the mission."

"NO!" Adrian cried. "I cannot complete the mission! I don't know where to begin, or where to end up! You've got to call me back through the Auratoss system!"

"I can't."

"You can!" Adrian cried louder.

"I can't . . . Adrian, you desperately need to complete this mission. Your friends still need you regardless of what happened to them; you're the only hope! You are the only one who spent enough time with Rhesus to truly know his plan! I know it will be difficult, but I am here; we will work through it together!"

Adrian felt more at ease. He nestled his back further into the rock and analyzed the words that Braddock had just spoken. He suddenly felt more vigorous, powerful, able to take on the task at hand; a smile crept across his face. What he would do, he did not know, but with he and Braddock as a team, they could accomplish anything!

A sharp stabbing pain suddenly pierced into Adrian's flesh just above his right knee. The image of Braddock quickly vanished, and Adrian turned his gaze downward to see a small man, no bigger than five inches tall, standing on his knee, holding a three and a half inch spear.

"You are my prisoner!" the tiny man yelled, aiming the spear at Adrian's head.

Adrian laughed at the sight.

"You won't be laughing when I get done with you!" the little man shouted, angrier than ever.

Adrian looked the small man over. His brown hair hung down past his shoulder, and he wore the skins of some kind of animal. His spear dangled in mid-air, ready to fly free any minute from the tight little grip of the man's tiny hand.

"Who are you, my little man?" Adrian asked politely.

The tiny man grounded his stance atop Adrian's knee. Adrian could barely feel the man's weight bearing down on his leg. "My name is Sir Cree-L! I am a great explorer and warrior, and you are my prisoner!"

Adrian couldn't help but like the little guy. "You're a great explorer, huh? Well, you just might be the answer to a prayer. I was talking to my friend Braddock and—"

"Who is this Braddock? I saw no one else!"

"He's my friend."

Cree-L Shrugged.

"He's in my head!"

Cree-L threw his spear to the ground in hopelessness and sat down on the crease in Adrian's pants. "So, you're looking for a great explorer, huh? And you want me to do it?!"

"Yeah, you look like you know your way around."

"I do. Did I not say that I was the greatest?"

"You did?" Adrian said.

"Well then, what's your final destination?"

"I'm not sure if it's a planet or a kingdom, but I'm trying to reach the palace of King Adam."

"Yes, I've heard of him. I can lead you to the city of Mallagone, that's as far as I can go!"

"You can't take me to the palace of King Adam? I thought you were a great explorer!"

"I am! But the path you seek to the palace of King Adam has already been explored, so there's no need for me to go that route!"

"You're no great explorer! You're just all talk!"

"Suit yourself!" the small man said, leaping from Adrian's leg, picking up his spear, and wandering off toward the trees.

"Okay! All right! Lead me to the city of Mailjen!" Adrian said, standing up.

"Mallagone!" Cree-L corrected him.

"Yes, Mallagone!" Adrian repeated. He followed Cree-L toward the thick woods and tried not to crush the small man beneath his enormous feet. Minutes passed and he felt as if he was chasing an insect; he trudged along very, very slowly. Surely if anyone was witnessing this trek, they would definitely be asking themselves why this man is plodding along through the grass at point-zero-zero-zero-one mile-an hour? "Did you want me to carry you?" Adrian asked.

"A great warrior does not need to be carried," the little man said confidently, bounding left and right among the dark green lawn blades.

"Well, as a great explorer, you can explore my pocket!" Adrian said, snatching the little guy from the ground and sliding him into his upper left shirt pocket. He quickened his pace and ignored Cree-L's cries of protest.

Adrian stopped as the bushes ahead, along the edge of the forest, rustled and swayed. A very curious-looking creature stumbled into view, waddled past Adrian, paying him no mind, and continued on without a care. The creature almost tripped on its wrinkles and thick folds of skin that dangled loosely from its frame. Rough, fine, coarse hair covered its entire body from head to toe, except its four thick, hooflike feet and the very end of its short snout.

"Has the bearer of the great explorer decided not to venture his chances in the forest?" Cree-L's muffled voice cried from within Adrian's pocket.

"No," Adrian answered.

"Then why have we stopped?" Cree-L said, poking his head out and observing the strange animal. An expression of worry quickly spread across his face, and the little man became horrified. "Get out of here!" he cried. "Get out of here, now!"

"Why?" Adrian responded.

Cree-L began to shake nervously and looked up at Adrian. "Let's get out of here, before that animal does something!"

"What! Him? He looks harmless enough!" Adrian said, watching the animal waddle its way through the lush grass.

"Do you not know what that animal is?"

"No."

"That's a reozzy! A distant cousin to the ciapaw! We've got to get out of here because he's walking bait!"

"What do you mean 'walking bait'?" Adrian asked.

Cree-L noticed the animal was some distance away now and felt more secure. "You see how that reozzy is walking in the middle of the open field?!"

"Yes."

"Well, wait and see!"

Adrian kept his eyes on the animal and waited eagerly. Nothing happened. Nothing but the shadow of a distant bird that swept across the grass in the field. The reozzy caught a glimpse of the shadow and slowed his pace; he began turning in a circle and laid down to wallow among the thick grasses, enticing the bird to draw nearer.

The bird of prey noticed the ruckus below and swooped lower; he converged quickly upon the animal with a terrible screeching cry of his victory and ripped his terrible talons into the flesh of his struggling victim, lifting him from the ground.

The reozzy began to grow, filling his oversized skin, until he grew to a size much larger than his predator; his skin pulled tightly over is muscular flesh, trapping the bird's huge talons that were still imbedded within. The bird of prey struggled to keep his victim airborne, but it was brutally pulled to the ground by the reozzy's sudden shift in weight.

The reozzy hit the ground, rolled over on top of is predator, and with a victory cry of his own, began to swallow the bird whole.

Adrian couldn't believe what he was witnessing; he had never seen the likes of this before! His eyes were transfixed in fascination as the reozzy continued to feed. At that moment the grass rustled behind him. Adrian turned with a snap of the neck and saw another massive reozzy standing on his hind legs, fully erect, and quickly bearing down on him. Adrian backed away and eyed the field and trees for any method of escape. The blood rushed from his face and fell to his stomach when he noticed, to his horror, he was surrounded, and more were coming out from the woods. They had smelled the scent of food and found the source, and they weren't going to leave until their elastic stomachs had their fill.

"Run!" Cree-L cried.

"There's no place to run!" Adrian returned, choking on his words.

The reozzy drew dangerously closer. It moaned with a deep rumbling growl that concluded with a high-pitched squeal. Adrian began to sweat profusely and continued his slow, uneasy progression away from the terrifying beast.

Keeping his eyes geared to the one animal, the other reozzies sensed his diversion and began to close in, in circular formation. The attack on the bird had been a trick; these animals obviously traveled together in a pack. And on bigger prey, when their short, hooflike legs were of no use, multiple jaws of very sharp teeth from surrounding animals had come in very handy.

The reozzy pressed forward unhesitatingly. He suddenly jolted from a shot that came from behind; quivering, he fell hard to the ground with a ghastly blow that knocked the very breath from him.

The other reozzies quickly retreated as thousands of tiny men poured from the safety of the thick trees and engulfed the huge animal with a fury of unbridled terror; they clamored up the beast's rough fur, stabbing him with sharp knives and spears. The reozzy wailed in pain and began throwing the little men into the air; the small men landed on the soft grass, picked themselves up, and poured back into battle.

Adrian didn't know what to do; he staggered around, then made sure Cree-L was safely in his pocket. He rolled up his sleeves and prepared to join the fight, when the beast cried out for the last time and tumbled to its doom.

The pigment of battle that stained the blood, coursing its way through each individual man, didn't stop at battles's end. They charged Adrian with spears and knives drawn, yelling and whooping, set on another kill.

Cree-L leapt from Adrian's pocket in a daring move, "STOP! STOP! He's my friend!" he yelled to the oncoming warriors.

The warriors continued their anger-filled rush.

"He's already my prisoner!" Cree-L yelled in another attempt to ease the onslaught.

The huge army came to a sudden halt, with spears still ready to fly. "Is what this man says is true?" one man yelled to Adrian from the front lines.

"It is," Adrian remarked humbly.

The army kept their spears ready and led Adrian six miles to the city of Mallagone. Small huts and villages lined the path on either side leading to the city; small women snatched their children from the yards and dashed inside the huts, to avoid them from being crushed by the giant. Adrian saw the city just ahead, its architecture simply astounded him. High rises and pillars ranged in all shapes and sizes, the highest standing five feet above his head and coming to rest just under the shelter of the overhead tree limbs. He reached the city and towered through it like a giant hot air balloon; the buildings featured tiny windows with the walls made of thick rock and mud. Adrian had seen buildings that were similar when he had helped Braddock do research on Indian ruins in Arizona. At the same time, the city was very futuristic at best; the outer shapes and designs were very eye pleasing, and with a few flashy lights, it would be no different from the buildings in a science-fiction film back on Earth.

Cree-L looked around the city from Adrian's pocket. "Ah, it's good to be home!" he said. "I've been gone for months, you know!"

Adrian looked down. "Wait a minute! When you said you were a great explorer and could lead me no farther than the city of Mallagone, all you meant was 'you were going home'!"

"Yeah, I've already had my adventure!"

"You probably got lost."

"For your information, my dear sir, I was seeking a prisoner for our city!"

"Honestly, how are you going to incarcerate me in these small buildings?"

Adrian was cut off when they came to a stop before a large group of official looking people. They did not sport the same skins and areas of flesh the others had, but rather, fine dark suits and olive green uniforms. The ambassador pierced through the crowd, wearing a bright red uniform and cape. He approached a wooden staircase that wound around until he stood atop a sturdy platform that was about as high as Adrian's navel.

"Why have you brought me here?" Adrian said, Keeping the prisoner mood alive. He knew deep down that this entire experience was a mockery.

The ambassador gave Cree-L a smug wave. "You have done well, my friend!" he motioned.

Cree-L waved back and climbed down from Adrian's pocket silently.

"Why have you brought me here?" Adrian repeated.

"What is your name, my lad?" the Ambassador said.

"Adrian!"

"That is a decent name!"

Adrian began to show signs of his impatience to play along with their little game.

"Why have we brought you here, you ask?" the ambassador said.

Adrian didn't respond, he just glared his fake discomforting glare.

"We are in need of your assistance! We wish to add to our city and extend farther to the south. A giant of your stature will easily complete the job within half a year."

"Are you aware that there is a war going on?!" Adrian harshly commented.

The ambassador grimaced. "We are aware of the war, but who or what we are subject to does not matter to our society. We live within the safety of the forest and do as we wish!"

"Can you be sure?!" Adrian said, throwing a suspicious look at him.

"Can you be sure that you will still be alive tomorrow if you do not end this charade!" the ambassador growled.

Adrian looked down. "What about supplies? Do you have enough food to support a giant like me for half a year?"

The ambassador turned away. "It is not your place to question our rations!" He hesitated briefly and turned back to Adrian. "But if your knowing will enable you to work more satisfactory, I will tell you. We are mainly vegetarian; we receive our fruits and vegetables from an old comrade who lives two days from here; he is just about your size. In fact, we are due to receive a shipment first thing tomorrow morning! His plan is simple; he can break off a piece of tappan fruit and enlarge it, break off another piece and repeat the same method. He never runs out, and we repay his services through the trade of our crafts."

Adrian couldn't believe what he was hearing. "He enlarges it?!" he said anxiously.

"Yes, it's a very simple process."

Adrian couldn't believe his good fortune. If this process could work on humans as well as fruit, he could possibly return home. "But what if . . ."

". . . That's enough for now," the ambassador interrupted. "I hope you enjoy sleeping outside! Sir Cree-L, please show our friend to his sleeping arrangements. He can begin work first thing tomorrow!"

"Yes, sir!" Cree-L snapped.

The next morning Adrian awoke to a very peculiar sound. He wiped the sleep from his eyes and peered over the small building that served as one of Mallagone's eating quarters. The sight he beheld knocked him from his half-asleep daze. Small men by the thousands rolled large, soft fruit on awkward wooden rollers. The fruit stood as high as the surrounding trees and pushed the limbs aside, making its way closer to the city. The fruit cleared the trees and came to a stop.

Adrian studied the fruit with a practiced eye and smelled the sweet fragrant odor of freshly picked fruit that drifted in the breeze. He suddenly grew very hungry; he jumped over the small buildings, approached the large delicate fruit, and touched the soft skin, his mouth watering. The nearer fruit had a soft, dark purple color, as opposed to the light green of the other. He had never tasted tappan fruit and longed to take a bite, to ease the pangs of hunger.

Cree-L walked along the cross board that withheld the uncommon fruit. "Isn't it amazing? It took the men two days to arrive with these fine delicacies; have you ever tried one?"

"No, but I'd love to!"

"We of course cannot partake of this fruit until after a day's work, but I brought you a small one to try." He handed Adrian a small, round, rich purple morsel that filled both of his hands and was the size of blueberry.

"Mmm, that is delicious!" Adrian said amusingly. "Can you take me to the source?"

"Oh, I can't do that! It would mean certain death. We had better get to work, then we will feast tonight!" Cree-L said, calmly walking off.

Adrian longed for another sweet tender bite; he loved the way the cool juices flowed down his parched throat, but he knew that such a treat would have to be earned from a full day of hard work.

12

Marrek's Mercantile

Adrian sat alone outside the city walls and looked up at the Moon Probe that illuminated the dark night sky and thinking about how he had abandoned his friends. Unfamiliar insects chirped and foraged out among the black obscurity, bringing the calming solitude of the night to a vibrant waking.

Cree-L appeared out of the darkness and sat down beside Adrian. "Some feast, do you not agree?!" he said.

"It was certainly something! I never could have imagined a simple fruit could have been prepared in so many ways."

"That's what we're best known for!" Cree-L paused and looked up at Adrian. "Do you wish to leave?"

"Oh, no, never! Your people have been more than generous to me; it's just that I have a mission to complete, and I want to return home where I belong."

"And that's why you want me to take you to visit Marrek?"

"Marrek?" Adrian asked. "Who is that?"

"Marrek is the old man who grows our fruit."

"Oh yes, right!" Adrian asserted. "Very much!"

Cree-L remained silent and Adrian knew he must change the subject in order to win over his sacred little friend. "So, uh, tell me about your people. How did they come to be here?"

Cree-L looked up at the bright yellow, glowing Moon Probe. "Forty-six Heavenly Guardians! Our ancestors were at one time, forty-six Heavenly Guardians! Huge balls of mud and rock had formed at the edge of the heaves, called planets. Our ancestors were sent forth to seek out the most beautiful one for the ruler Galla, for which this planet is named after."

"So, the name of this planet is Galla; very appropriate!" Adrian said.

"Thank you! The Heavenly Guardians then set about to carve Galla's face into the rock and mud as the highest of tributes. When Galla heard of their plans, he ordered that the planet should be set aside for his people to enjoy. Three heavenly messengers were sent bearing gifts that would help turn the planet Galla into a garden: Dreams, heart, and fire. Our forty-six ancestors utilized the gifts for their posterity, and we still use those gifts in our souls today," Cree-L concluded.

"You know, we believe in Heaven where I come from. That's a weird coincidence! Only, we refer to Heavenly Guardians, as Guardian Angels."

"Angels? I've never heard of that word!"

"That's just the word we describe of the beings that watch over us," Adrian said.

"That *is* a coincidence!" Cree-L reflected.

Adrian looked once again at the eerie beauty of the Moon Probe that cast its glorious light over this beautiful world.

Cree-L stuttered softly. "I . . . I . . . I will take you to see Marrek."

"You will?!" Adrian said joyfully.

"Yes, after the completion of our city."

"It will be too late then! I must complete my mission now! I assure you, when my mission is completed, I will find reinforcements to help build your city! But it is imperative that I leave, now! Tonight!"

"Tonight?" Cree-L choked.

"What's it going to be?" Adrian begged. "I can't do it without you, you must come with me!"

Cree-L's response was delayed by a long siren that reverberated from the city. He dashed off once again into the night, then returned minutes later. "That was our commander, Ac-nine. He has just received word that there will be another attack on the moon probe."

"By who?" Adrian asked.

"I heard it was the planet Varnet. They will have commenced attack by the time we get back to the city; come on!"

"We can't, don't you see!" Adrian shouted.

"See what? I know that if they destroy the Moon Probe this time, the force of the blow will do who-knows-what to this planet!"

"They might destroy it, and they might not! I've been inside that Moon Probe, and I know that it will take a lot more power than one planet can resource! It is part of my mission to rally the planets together in one united strength!"

Huge fireballs pierced the night sky in sequence and began bombarding the outer crust of the Moon Probe. The enormous moon didn't budge or shake in its orbit. Adrian was awestruck by the sight, as artillery cracked and lit up the night sky with colorful fireworks.

"It has begun," Cree-L said stately.

Adrian looked over his newfound little friend, hoping for a positive response to his plea.

"If I were to take you to Marrek, it would truly help?" Cree-L said.

"It would be a start, I'm at a dead end!"

Cree-L stared up at the battle raging in the sky and pondered the situation. "Okay," he said finally, "I will take you to see Marrek. Let's gear up and leave immediately!"

"I knew you wouldn't let me down!" Adrian cheered.

The trek to Marrek's domain was a long and tedious one. They reached the crest of a mountain by the dawn of the second day and peered down into a valley that was a virtual Eden. Giant fruit covered the ground for as far as the eye could see.

"Let's make our way down that long gorge down there," Cree-L suggested.

They made their way down and through the luscious fruit until they reached the center of the valley and stood before a large mercantile. A few other customers had arrived earlier and were pressing and smelling the fruit, looking for the freshest deal.

"Let's go inside," Cree-L said.

The door was unlocked. Adrian entered and found himself in the middle of a bustle, as employees busied themselves preparing for a good day's work. "May I help you?" one spoke out.

"Yes, we are looking for Marrek," Adrian said.

"Right this way," the salesperson said, motioning for them to follow.

Marrek stepped out from the back room, giving another employee instructions for the day.

"Sir, this gentleman says he's looking for you," the employee said, not noticing Cree-L in Adrian's pocket.

Marrek turned his attention to Adrian, and the two workers disappeared back to work. "What can I do for you?" he asked.

Cree-L made himself known. "I'll take it from here," he interrupted.

Marrek gave Cree-L a wistful glance. "Ahh, Cree-L! Protector of the fruit, how are we this fine morning?"

"Yeah, yeah, laugh it up," Cree-L joked back. "My friend here wishes to see the fruit-growing machine."

"Oh, I can't do that. We've had too many saboteurs trying to get their dirty little hands on that machine and ruin business," Marrek said.

Adrian fully understood and told Marrek his plans to visit King Adam, Marrek wished him well and agreed to let Adrian see the machine when he had completed his mission, after some security measures could be established.

"Do you think the machine could be used to enlarge humans?" Adrian asked.

Marrek was startled by the question and paused to think. "I suppose in theory it could, but I wouldn't try it."

Adrian would try it, He would return and try it because it was the only chance he knew he truly had left, but for now, he had more important things to do.

Marrek called for his apprentices, Doblin and Suca, to help lead Adrian to the king and avoid, if possible, any undermining Die-cell raids. Doblin was a muscular, golden metallic humanoid with sharp leonine features that demanded respect, which was in deep contrast to his counterpart, Suca, whose small grayish-brown, hairy body and sweet innocent face made him appear all too trustworthy.

Doblin stepped forward. "I believe I know the shortest route," his robotic voice echoed. "Diabolis has captured most of our transport systems, so we'll have to travel on foot."

"Let's do it," Adrian said eagerly.

They quickly gathered the needed supplies that they would need for the journey, along with a complete arsenal of weapons for protection. Marrek issued Adrian several delicious morsels of his famous fruit, and the small crew set out across the great valley.

More curious looking creatures had arrived and began prodding, poking, and kicking the fruit, as Marrek's staff continued to busy themselves with customer relations.

Adrian couldn't help but notice the way Doblin walked. His powerful joints creaked like gears, causing his heavy feet to impact the ground with great force. He was almost a flesh-covered robot that could easily fool any living creatures into believing he was all flesh and blood from the day he was born and not the man-made creation he was. Suca had trouble keeping up with Doblin's long stride. He ran up from behind, placing himself somewhat behind Doblin, his short little legs struggling to keep pace.

Doblin stopped.

Suca's quickness caused him to collide into Doblin's surefooted structure, bringing him to a complete stop as well.

Doblin stared past the barrier of purple and green fruit ahead. "Die-cells!" he said. "This way!"

The Die-cells stormed around the large fruit, recognizing Adrian from their 'missing persons' identity scanners. "Halt!" they shouted. Follow me, I know where to go!" Doblin beckoned. His thick cumbersome walk suddenly altered into a solid smooth motion, as he darted around one massive fruit after another, leaving Adrian and Suca far behind. Adrian's only hope of finding his way was to follow the deeply imbedded footprints that Doblin had left behind in the thick soil.

Fruit exploded all around from the Die-cells' gunfire.

Adrian leapt around the last piece of fruit at the far end of the valley, just in time to see Doblin mount a motorbike and disappear into the sky along a thing roller coaster track. He had seen Braddock drive motorcycle lots of times, but he had never driven one himself.

"Halt!" the Die-cells cried again

Adrian had no time to look back, he had to go. He jumped on the nearest bike, followed by Suca, who leapt onto a bike on the next track over.

Adrian throttled the bike's engine hard, and suddenly feeling the sensation of weightlessness, he took off into the sky and sailed over the mountain. He felt for a moment that he had no control over the bike's un-temperate movement, racing against the wind with nothing below him for miles.

A small unit of angry Die-cell soldiers were in desperate pursuit, revving up their own bikes to full throttle and taking off after Adrian. They grew angrier and fiercer by the minute as he continued to elude them.

Adrian—panic-stricken-thrust more power into his rail-cycle's engine and leaned into the sharp curve. The bike straightened out and dipped into a vertical drop, ripping under dangerous archways through the canyon walls. His boosters roared, shaking the treacherous rocks high over head; he banked left and began to feel the thrill of the race.

The Die-cells, who were accustomed to such bikes, fired their guns, forgetting about the wind resistance that repelled the electric bolts of red laser fire away from Adrian.

Cree-L, who had never been a praying man, suddenly became one. He crouched down deep in Adrian's shirt pocket, grabbed the loose material tightly, and hung on for dear life.

The rail-cycle sped through another great valley, around jagged edged mountains, shallow steep canyons and over heart-wrenching drops in a series of twisting, winding curves and loops at great speeds. Adrian insisted on more power, entering another trench that narrowed and deepened; he bore down on the thrusters harder and exploded through the gap onto the open flats, engines screaming. The rail-bike was beginning to speak to him. He could sense what was about to happen to him over the next hill by the vibrations and the rush of wind that seemed to whisper into his ear.

Suca flashed by on a rail-bike of gleaming metal and disappeared ahead along with Doblin on there alternate tracks. Adrian cleared another mountain and gasped in horror at the giant loop that shot upwards, penetrating the clouds. His rail-cycle followed the track steadily, not reducing speed by any fluctuation; he sped upward, seeing nothing but sky—his stomach sank, as his bike rode the top upside down, then plunged downward. He could feel his rail-cycle rampantly picking up speed, and he knew the worst was yet to come. He leveled off at the base and quickly gathered his senses; ahead, the track came to an abrupt end, hanging dangerously out over a massive canyon of colorful rock. Inside, Adrian could feel his innards retreat, but the rail-bike continued on at greater speeds. He tightened his grip on the crossbars and prepared for the worst. His bike left the track and flew through the air, the rubber less tires still spinning. The view was magnificent, but Adrian's concerns were not on beauty; the track on the other side drew closer and Adrian maneuvered the rail-cycle as best he could to hit the track square, the air not adding any support for steering.

The rail-cycle finally landed on the track, snapping securely, and continued on without varying speed. It raced on, whipping through columns of an ancient city that had been reduced to rubble, and passing statues of ancient dignitaries that had once been. Outside the fallen ruins was the modern city of Arguello, where 'droids, Sebull Stormers, and two-headed magpeens raced from their well-lit buildings to cheer the racers on. Adrian caught momentary glimpses of the blurred figures as his rail-bike swerved under a bridge.

Doblin and Suca were ahead, and Adrian soon caught up with them. They soared as a team, over lakes, leaving ripples in the water from the force of their cycles; over trees with elevated limbs that brushed a few Die-cells crashing, bikes and all, to the bottom of the forest; through twisting channels low and tight, and across ground to more flats beyond—trying to put more distance between themselves and the Die-cells.

The Die-cells were having none of it, and began gaining ground as the seconds flew.

Adrian drew back power to his rail-cycle, as he neared an upcoming gorge—too much power and he'd be in trouble. He veered right and burst into the shadows. Doblin and Suca were watching his back through the darkness. Deadly rock flew past in a delicate array of patterns and shapes, disorienting his vision, making the track and turns ahead difficult to distinguish. He closed his eyes tightly, as his rail-bike carried him down another channel and began to spin ferociously on the twisted track, as if he were sliding down a corkscrew—his eyes flew open. He witnessed Doblin and Suca merging ahead into the brief darkness of more shadows. His rail-bike tilted tightly sideways, sucking him back around powerful curves, which took his breath away, forcing the air from his lungs.

The Die-cells' black rail-cycles edged forward, rubbing metal wheel upon metal wheel, trying to make Adrian flip from the track and smash into the rock walls.

Adrian gained speed on the next downward drop. He emerged into the light, forced the throttle roaring and streaking after his friends, away from the Die-cells. He made a vertical leap straight up along the track, losing the rest of the Die-cells in a cloud of exhaust.

Doblin and Suca made daring leaps onto alternate tracks and vanished. Could he do the same? His rail-bike slammed downward again; he pulled back on the steering and eased off the track, landing on the rails his friends had. He looked back briefly and watched the pursuing Die-cells pass, headed for the thick trees. He then loosened his grip on the throttle, cutting off fuel to the engine and coasted along with his friends on the steady, smooth off-ramp.

The Die-cells would surely find another way around, so they had to constantly keep moving.

13

The Land of Suca

The whole planet began to shake. Adrian knew the separation was seventy-five percent complete; they had to stop Diabolis, now.

The crusaders rode their rail-cycles through the unusually shaped mountains and cliffs. Music began to fill the air, and the team passed through the V-formation in the rock and entered into the colonies of Benoit. The colonies stretched for miles; their buildings were carved from the hollow Kinmont Mountain range.

Suca stopped, his rail-bike teetering on the thin rail. "This be my home," he said.

"What is that strange music?" Adrian asked, raising an eyebrow.

"That be the dance to chase the bad omen of Diabolis away," Suca said, in his bizarre, hard to understand accent.

Adrian sat wordlessly.

"We need to go. It be long travel to Majesty Adam," Suca continued.

Doblin's thick, heavy metallic voice contradicted Suca. "No, we stay here tonight."

"We best not! Get caught up in dancing—party!" Suca retorted.

"No, we stay here tonight!" Doblin repeated, seeming a bit bothered.

Adrian knew there was not much time left and had to stand up in Suca's defense. "I believe Suca knows what is best, considering this is his home."

Doblin turned and looked at Adrian. "Too dangerous: it will be getting dark soon."

Adrian looked at Suca, then back at Doblin. He did not want to get on the bad side of Doblin and risk losing his help. He looked down and reluctantly nodded.

"You respond foolishly," Suca said.

Doblin said nothing. He revved his rail-bike and proceeded down a thin green rail that branched off from the main railway system. Suca followed close behind, and the two disappeared once again down the dramatic slope. Adrian sat there, listening to the idle growl of his rail-bike; the light over the colonies slowly grew dimmer as the electric sun slowly set behind the Kinmont Mountains that Suca called home. Had he made the right choice? He wished he could ride the rail-cycle as far as it could take him, but who knew what is on the other side of the colonies? For now, he would have to trust Doblin's decision.

"Nobody asked me what I thought," Cree-L said, poking his head out of Adrian's pocket.

"Well, what do you think?" Adrian asked.

"I think we should follow Doblin's plan."

"Oh, you're so brave," Adrian said, kicking his bike into motion and sailing downhill into the music.

"Can I have my own rail-bike?" Cree-L asked.

The track ended and Adrian parked his bike, walked down the gentle sloping pathway, and entered into the rich, soul-stirring music that lifted up from the colonies. Excited, short, fuzzy mammals, similar to Suca, danced on either side of the rocky road that divided the large mountain lodges.

The mammals were called Simmels. Their people had been forced from their city of Margon by the battle of the same name, one thousand years ago. They fled into the mountains for protection where their innovation persevered, transforming the quiet lifeless rocks and cliffs into a thriving metropolitan populace. They irrigated the water that trickled from the mountaintops that housed some five million Simmels quite contentedly.

They had begun their ritual dances the day Diabolis's power became a true threat praying to their god to take the music that they sent and use it to touch what was left of Diabolis's soul.

Adrian cut through the crowd. The Simmels stood as high as his waist and continuously bumped into him, maintaining their rough yet sleek dance moves. More Simmels poured out of cave-like entrances to join the festivities, spilling over temporary barriers that had been set up for crowd control; some would leap from small round windows and slide down a cable to the ground that was suspended only by a thin pulley; Adrian noticed one that rode a thin copper hover-disc that was thrust into the air by a quick burst of steam. The small creature squealed in delight. Leaping through the air into the awaiting arms of his friends below. More Simmels slid down stair banisters, while others raced through the crowd feeding their faces with rare meats and other delicacies.

The noise level began to reach a deafening level, as the small Simmels commenced jumping up and down, sending a rippling wave of fur through the valley of colonies.

The silver haze of the giant electric sun cast its last rays over the mountaintops, preparing to bring the day to a close and revealing the silhouettes of some unwanted guests. Die-cells. The Die-cells secured their ropes to the rock and repelled down the steep cliffs with military precision.

The electric sun disappeared, giving way to the lost darkness of the night. The Simmels could sense the repulsive presence of the Die-cells and began to flee back to their homes in a chaotic mass of high-pitched screams.

Adrian stood motionless as the crying Simmels poured around him like a rock in a river. The force was too great. He thundered down and felt the thousands of tiny feet scurrying over his entire body, while the small creatures ran and tripped in terror. Adrian landed face down and jolted his shoulder upwards to avoid crushing Cree-L. His hand instinctively swung to his upper pocket to embrace Cree-L from danger, but felt nothing—Cree-L was gone. Adrian panicked and double checked, as if he overlooked Cree-L huddling down deep in his pocket. Nothing. He frantically searched the ground, and fighting, stumbled back to his feet. He looked over the crowd and caught a glimpse of Doblin heading back deeper into the colonies straight for the Die-cells, surely Suca was with him. There was nothing more he could do for Cree-L, he had to let him go and pray he would be all right.

The crowd of Simmels briefly parted, and Adrian gained a few extra feet. He pushed a few of the unsuspecting creature's aside and followed Doblin and Suca into one of the multiplex mountain housing units. Everything on the inside differed vastly from the outward appearance. It almost appeared like a modern luxury hotel, with thick, lush carpet extending over the floor. He followed Doblin and Suca up a delicately carve wooden flight of stairs, listening to them bicker all the way.

"I did indeed inform you that we could not stay the night!" Suca shouted, leading Doblin up one flight of stairs after another.

"Where then are we going?" Doblin responded, traipsing along behind.

"To get me supplies!" Suca said, running down the hallway on floor one sixty-seven. He burst through the door of his small living quarters and ran about his room, throwing everything he could get his small fuzzy hands on, into an already-full blue trunk.

"Oh, no. We're not taking that monstrosity with us!" Doblin complained. "We don't have the room or the time to haul around a big, useless, blue trunk!"

Suca insisted, chirping all kinds of explicit language that Adrian had never heard before. He then snatched up the trunk, dragged it past Doblin, and hauled it down the stairs, with Doblin complaining all the way. Minutes passed and the arguing duo reached the bottom of the stairs. Doblin would have to put his food down. He leapt around Suca and sat his powerful weight down on the trunk, insuring that his little friend could pull it no farther.

Adrian watched the two with amusement. At that moment, Braddock's virtual image suddenly appeared. "We are restrained to short time limits, which I deeply regret," he said. "Are there any updates?"

"A few," Adrian responded. He brought Braddock up-to-date while walking outside and finding himself in the middle of a deadly Die-cell advance.

"There he is!" one of the Die-cell commanders yelled, gesturing his gun through the air for his alliance to pursue.

Adrian spent no time in judging the distance of the approaching enemy. He peered through the vague imprint of Braddock's holographic face for any obstacles in his path and took off running, pumping his arms and legs, using his entire body to reap all the benefits that he could in his retreat.

The small colony crossroads were virtually vacated. No Simmels could be seen or heard anywhere. Bombs exploded all around as Adrian flew down the pathways, his adrenaline racing. He ran deeper into the loud music and was blown from the side from an unseen force that swept his feet out from under him. His hands were scuffed up from the small rocks—he jerked his head up—the image of Braddock was still there.

"Are you all right?" Braddock asked, not fully understanding what was going on. "Can you hear me? Are you all right?"

Adrian said nothing. He looked painfully through Braddock to see what had caused the sudden blast. "It's the sound system," he said, covering his ears from the music that continued to blare. "It's the sound system, but it looks like the small satellite dish that we had on the roof of our house."

Braddock suddenly realized Adrian was being chase and had no weapons to protect himself with. An idea popped into his mind. "Adrian, retrieve the sound system. I think I've heard of such innovative devices."

Adrian pulled on the device, freeing it from the ground. "Now what?" he yelled.

"Shut it off."

"How?"

"Cut the cable!"

The sound began piercing Adrian's ears. He squinted his eyes and quickly buried the vociferous gadget into the dirt. "There isn't any cable! It's receiving transmission by remote!"

Braddock had no time to pause and think. "Pull the back cover off!"

Adrian found the small gray control box on the back and pried the latch off with a rock. "Okay?" he said, swinging the tiny door open and looking in to see the small mess of tangled wires.

"Pullout the 'feedback' wire; it should be the big wire that is connected directly to the main dish!"

Adrian located it, wrapped his fingers around it, and yanked it loose. The music fell silent. "Got it! Go on!" he said.

"I can't believe it! They have virtually the same ideas and innovation we do here. I think I can definitely alter this system! Even though it is a brand new technology!" Braddock confided.

Adrian was just surprised that creatures as ignorant looking as the Simmels could even think of such a lucrative sound system. "Now what?" he cried, knowing time was against him.

"Okay, switch the inaudibility cable and the sibilant cable; they should be the wires on the far outsides!"

Adrian followed Braddock's instructions and responded when he had completed the task. "Okay, got it!"

"Reverse the chip on the bottom right-had corner one hundred and eighty degrees. This should direct the sound away from you!"

"Okay, go ahead!" Adrian said.

"Now just simply reconnect the 'feedback' wire to the main dish, and you're finished!"

Adrian did so. He then closed the back cover and re-locked the latch securely.

Braddock continued, "Turn the distort knob all the way off, and when you wish to use the dish, just turn the power switch on!"

Adrian looked at Braddock. "What am I using the sound dish for?"

Braddock's image abruptly disappeared like a television turning off.

The Die-cells stormed up and surrounded Adrian in an unshielded array of deadly force, with guns aimed. Adrian thrashed the sound dish upwards as a shield. Gunfire exploded, ricocheting off the fragile concave dish and exploded back in the Die-cells' faces. Adrian slid his fingers nervously to the base of the sound system and flipped the power on. The sound thundered from the dish in a powerful steady stream of unvarying sound waves, knocking the Die-cells back. His finger held tightly to the power switch, and with a single flick, he quickly cut the power.

The Die-cells were stunned but quickly re-gathered. Adrian wasted no more time; he released another stream of sound that hit the Die-cells like a brick wall, then cut the power again.

One lone Die-cell soldier remained standing. He secured his gun in his hand and emitted a terrible translucent jutting ray that sliced past Adrian's right ear. Adrian spun around, activated the power again, and jerked upwards, carrying the shocked soldier high into the sky. The Die-cell screamed, as Adrian turned the 'distort' knob to high and then to low, while watching and laughing as the sound waves engulfed the scared soldier, dropping him, then causing him to soar.

Adrian then turned the 'distort' knob completely off. The intense sound waves pulsated from the small system and levitated the soldier at a height greater than the mountain-tops. Adrian laughed until he had his fill, then let the man drop in small bursts until he safely reached the ground.

The Die-cells regained formation and charged at Adrian. Adrian picked the lone Die-cell soldier up again, and with a quick athletic movement, swung him into the oncoming raid, knocking down ten Die-cells or more.

The angry army did not slow their advance; they rushed toward Adrian with a rage of fury. He danced through the crowd, pelting the soldiers with quick clips of sound, insuring no Die-cell had time to discharge his weapon. Adrian knew he was doomed when more Die-cells filled the small valley and quickly formed a circle around him. He held fast to his weapon and beliefs, and he battled on.

Thousands of Simmels with anger-filled swollen hearts stampeded through the darkness to Adrian's rescue, bearing fierce weapons of various sizes and types. They splashed into the Die-cells, fighting for their homes and their land. They would not be defeated. It was war, and Adrian was right in the middle of it.

One Die-cell soldier thrashed around like a man possessed, flinging his arms through the air, and rotating like a demon direct from the underworld. The soldier spun closer and Adrian noticed Cree-L wrapped around the man's head, throwing quick, tiny, soft punches. Adrian had to chuckle. He threw the sound system into gear and knocked the Die-cell to the ground. He then ran over, and without stopping, scooped Cree-L up and continued on through the battle, throwing harsh bolts and punches along the way. He saw Doblin and Suca ahead and and handed the small sound dish to a very shocked and bewildered Simmel, then reached his two friends, who were already on their way out of the colonies.

Adrian looked at Suca. "Your people are the best!" he shouted above the gunfire.

"Me know," Suca replied.

Adrian took a hold of the blue trunk and hastened the procession, with Cree-L riding on top.

Doblin marched ahead, leading the way. "We will find a safe haven for tonight so you mortals can rest," he said.

"Agreed!" Adrian said, in fresh assertion.

14

Suca's Trunk

Diabolis stood in the middle of the control center, surrounded on each side by his trustworthy generals, captains, and respected authoritarians. They deeply pondered their next move, studying accurate star charts, represented by colorful rainbow bubbles that had been encoded with blue holographic numbers to identify each individual planet—the final destiny of each living orb.

General Tracer, Diabolis's newly appointed general, entered into the room and walked nonchalantly over to the large, smooth, black table that stretched out throughout most of the room. He gave a brief glance at the huge bubbles that calmly floated in position over the table, then turned to Diabolis. "We have the green planet of Quinn in tow and will soon capture the red," he reported.

"Good," Diabolis said, from the other side of the table. "That makes it official. I will officially be the ruler of our new galaxy in five Harmoroon days." He turned to the Major. "Let's make it an event! This is truly something to celebrate!"

"I have anticipated your thinking, your Highness," the Major said, felicitously. "We have something special planned for you on Harmoroon-3."

"Good," Diabolis said again, reaching across the table and popping each bubble, one after another.

* * *

Adrian awoke the next morning on the cold, wet cave floor that Doblin had found the night before. The bright, white hues of the electric sun flickered in the cave entrance, announcing its new arrival. He looked around. Cree-L slept soundly on top of the trunk; his deep bothersome snoring filled the cave like a hibernating bear that was entrapped in a terrible nightmare.

Suca tossed and turned in the corner and rolled into a sitting position. He looked back at Adrian and wiped the sleep from his eyes wearily. "This be morning?" his tired vocal cord gruffed.

"This be morning," Adrian responded. "How did you sleep last night?"

Suca stretched his short furry legs. "Obey-dobie."

"You mean, Okey-dokey," Adrian replied.

"No, mean, Obey-dobie! Nowhere near Okey-dokey."

Adrian dropped the subject, not knowing if what Suca was referring to was better or worse. "Where is Doblin?" he asked.

"He no need sleep; he stand watch outside."

Cree-L suddenly jerked, hit the hard trunk with a swift blow, screamed in pain, and continued his deep sleep.

"Weird friend you have," Suca said, not taking his eyes off Creek-L.

"One of the fiercest warriors in the land," Adrian said, in amusement.

"Indeed," Suca said, standing up.

Adrian looked at the small fuzzy man and again tried to determine if that statement had been true or sarcastic. He slowly stood up and walked out of the cave, feeling a gentle gust of fresh morning air that blew soothingly against his face. He breathed it in deep. Doblin stood down the slope a bit, looking out over the fog that had settled in the valley below. Adrian cleared his morning voice. "Is there anything good to eat around here?!" he called to Doblin.

"We've brought small pieces of tappan fruit, but we will eat those later," Doblin responded.

Suca staggered from the cave, dragging and scraping his humongous blue trunk harshly over the rock floor. Doblin walked back up the slope, grunting a few chosen words under his breath, and took hold of the handle, shaking it wildly. Cree-L steadied himself by placing his hands flat on the trunk.

Adrain set out down the mountain. No marked path could be seen. He led his friends winding down and around, avoiding loose gravel and cliff edges. The small crew traveled for hours and Doblin grew tired and angrier at having to haul around the heavy trunk by the minute. They wound around mountain after mountain, twisting and turning, climbing one embankment after another. Exhausted, the tiny group stopped to rest high atop a steep trench. Doblin continued, dragging the trunk closer to the cliff's edge.

"No!" Suca cried, grasping at his would-be lost possession.

Cree-L leapt for his life, as Doblin threw the trunk into mid-air with his mighty strength, sending it plummeting down into the dark abyss.

Suca rushed to the edge, laid flat on his belly, and looked down into the deep gulch, but to no avail. Everything he owned was gone. He turned back to Doblin with sadness swelling in his eyes. "Why you do such thing?" he quivered.

Doblin looked into his tiny face sternly. "We haven't much time and it slowed us down."

Suca scampered away.

Adrian picked Cree-L up off the ground, and returned him to his upper pocket, and followed after. He found Suca around the curve of the slope, leaning against a huge, towering rock that completely matched his fur.

"That be everything I own," Suca said, trying to hold back the tears.

"I know," Adrian said in a calm consoling voice.

At that moment, something suddenly brushed against Adrian's leg. He slowly turned, then panicked. It was a reozzy. Adrian leapt away in a burst of impulse.

Suca's mood lightened, and he rushed to the animal in a fit of glee. "Me take that back—not everything I own!"

Adrian was stunned. "He . . . he's yours?!"

"Yes, his name is Skoura!" Suca turned to the animal. "How you find me way out here?"

The beast bristled, flaring his nostrils. His thick, light brown hair stood on end, and he slowly waddled toward Adrian. Adrian scaled the smooth rocks without knowing how he'd done it and looked back to see the creature pawing his short stubby legs against the hard rock in an attempt to climb up after. "Call him off!" Adrian cried.

"Skoura!" Suca shouted.

The beast appeared to grow angrier, clawing deeper into the rock.

"He be liking you!" Suca called to Adrian.

"I'm not so sure!"

"Of course! If he not, he would grow and eat you!"

"What am I supposed to do?!" Adrian called back.

"Come down. Let him get to know you!"

"Are you sure?"

"Me sure!"

Adrian hesitantly climbed down. The reozzy grunted and began smelling his feet. The beast stumbled forward and began pressing his snout against Adrian's legs, pressing him and trying to figure out his limitations. Adrian held fast, praying the creature would not take a bite out of him or swallow him whole.

"See," Suca said, "he be liking you."

Adrian looked at the light brown reozzy. "I don't think he's eaten in a couple of days."

"He no need to eat for couple of weeks."

"When did you feed him last?"

"The morning I left the mercantile. I fed him pounds of tappan fruit."

Adrian turned his fearful gaze to Suca. "Oh, great! A vegetarian meat eater. I get the impression he's not satisfied."

"He loves it!" Suca said cheerfully.

"Yeah," Adrian responded, with a tone of complete uncertainty.

The reozzy grunted harshly one last time and waddled his way back to Suca.

Doblin walked slowly into view, then stopped. He eyed the creature over precariously, then stepped forward a couple of steps.

"Me have protection now, you brute!" Suca said, trying to place the reozzy between himself and Doblin.

Adrian could tell that the creature wanted no part of the situation because a humanoid such as Doblin would probably be too much for him to chew. Doblin calmly walked past with a confident stride and continued on down the mountain. The beast snapped briskly at his heels, but dared not sink his teeth into the thick flesh, for fear of his own termination. The reozzy pulled back sharply and took his place alongside his master like a devoted puppy, and followed the threatening crew with eyes wide and alert.

The unique team headed down at a quickened pace, due to the heavy, confining pull of gravity. They had left the colony of Simmels long ago and now just looked over a vacant valley of empty cuestas and mountains that rose from the ground like giant pyramids.

Doblin marched along, leading the way like a proud commander, his head held high. Adrian believed in his ability fully and was now more likely to listen to what he had to say, rather than Suca and his psychotic pet. Doblin cut to the left and entered a deep, overwhelming trench that towered over them on each side, above them only sky. The canal sliced to a thin course until the team found themselves walking single file through the enclosing rocks.

The canal seemed endless, and Adrian was growing tired of the monotony. He suddenly spotted something up ahead; it wasn't much, just a small overhang, a bridge of sorts. Something was sitting on both the right and left sides of the channel.

"Look!" Suca shouted. "My trunk!"

Suca was right. They were well below the ridge that Doblin had thrown it from. It had obviously landed securely, balancing delicately on each side of the canal, upside-down. The sided of the trench lowered as they neared the trunk, until it dangled a couple of feet over their heads.

"Help me get it down!" Suca begged.

Doblin sternly hesitated.

"I'll help you," Adrian said. He firmly took hold of the small man and boosted him into the air. Suca quickly grasped the wooden handle that was fastened to the top of the trunk and dangled in mid-air, kicking his tiny legs and tugging furiously to loosen one side and bring it tumbling down.

Adrian watched the humorous spectacle and had to try something else. He leapt from the ground, slid his thin fingers over the smooth wooden bar latch, and thrashed his body weight to the left. The trunk still didn't budge.

The reozzy watched his master struggle. He bore his sharp teeth that were embedded in his hard, black gums, lunged at Adrian and caught his deadly teeth in the cuff of his pants, and whipped around like a mad, wild dog.

Doblin could see his friends were getting nowhere; they needed more strength. He walked to the other side of the trunk, jumped, and took hold of the other handle. The trunk moved. Doblin gave the trunk another tug. It moved again, then stopped. He tried once more. The trunk crept toward him, then picked up speed. It slid down the two stone high-rises like a rail-bike on its track. Soon, it was flying along the trench, scuffing its lid on the rock, and soaring at an incredible rate of speed.

Adrian tried desperately to shake the horrid reozzy loose from the grip he had on his pants leg. Now was the time he could make it look like an accident. The reozzy was bent on murder; his jaw asserted hundreds of pounds of pressure and would never turn loose for anything. He continued to thrash around uncontrollably, barely missing the rock walls that flew past.

The trunk rocketed farther down the mountain as the gentle slope grew steeper and steeper. It flew around long, dramatic curves and quick, sudden drops. The wind whipped over Adrian's body; the reozzy's weight pulled down hard on his leg. He could feel his grip slowly breaking away from the smooth handle; soon it would be just him and the insane reozzy stranded together out in the middle of nowhere. He stepped on the reozzy's head and pushed himself up enough to tighten his grip on the bar.

The trench abruptly ended and the trunk was sent flying through the air. It crashed to the ground, sending everyone rolling in every direction. Suca came to a stop and grabbed Skoura around the neck before the reozzy could reestablish his balance.

Adrian stood up. "That is one crazy animal! Keep him away from me!" he shouted, backing away as far as he could.

Suca gently scratched Skoura's head. "Course he grabbed you! He no want to be left behind!"

"No, he's just plain crazy!"

Suca ignored Adrian's cries of protest and continued stroking Skoura tenderly. "Where we be anyway?" he asked.

Doblin paused, trying to find the appropriate words. "We are on course," he said, pausing again. "But, I believe I owe you an apology, your, uh . . . your trunk saved us I don't know how many miles and how much time."

"Indeed!" Suca said.

"I am sorry," Doblin continued, in his steady metallic voice. "I shouldn't have said what I did back there."

"You be forgiven!" Suca said, turning loose of the reozzy.

Adrian froze. But the powerful animal had seemed to forget about the entire incident and calmly and awkwardly walked behind his master.

Something about the land seemed different. The group crossed over the next ridge, and Adrian beheld an awesome sight. The land stretched for miles, with gentle sloping arches and smooth curves that were made out of a thick, pink, plastic-like material. Spanning the smooth surface were thick bumps that were as big around as both Adrian's hands put together. The team entered onto the strange bit of earth, their feet slipping wildly beneath them. They approached and tried to climb the first small hill, only to find themselves sliding back down. They tried once more, but with the same result.

"This be no good," Suca exclaimed.

"Don't give up so soon," Adrian said. "We made it this far, we can make it the rest of the way."

"Me not sure," Suca remarked again.

Doblin looked over the bizarre textured land. "We need to take a short break and try again."

"Yeah, we need something to enlighten our spirits," Adrian said.

"How about a song?" Suca honed in.

"Okay, do you know any?" Adrian asked. "Many!" Suca took in a deep breath and let out an ear-piercing squeal. Adrain felt the ground beneath his feet vibrate and watched Suca's trunk slide across the land toward the hill.

"Do that again," Adrian said.

Suca took in another breath and turned loose another terrible vocal arrangement. His trunk climbed the hill and approached the top.

"Okay, stop!" Adrian yelled, before the trunk disappeared over the hill and they wouldn't be able to retrieve it.

Suca brought his trumpeting voice to an abrupt end. The trunk suddenly stopped, slowly slid back down, and coasted to a stop.

"All right, everybody on!" Adrian shouted.

Doblin looked at him. "On what?" he said.

"You don't get it? We're going to ride the trunk over the hills!"

"Are you crazy?" Doblin said.

Suca scampered to the trunk and took his place on top. "This be fun!" he said, dragging Skoura up to sit beside him.

Doblin looked at the large trunk, then back at Adrian. "I don't believe it could carry all our weight."

Adrian said nothing. *"There's always someone who doubts everything,"* he thought to himself. He walked over the smooth, hard bumps that covered the land and sat on top of the trunk with Suca between him and the reozzy.

Doblin followed hesitantly and sat on the front. "If this should work, how do you suggest I steer this thing?"

"I don't know, but we'll figure it out!" Adrian said. He turned to Suca, "Okay, teach us a song."

"This song be called 'Ander', it be old festive song of me people. It go like this: My roon of min say kay!—Now you try!"

Adrian repeated the words perfectly and was quite content with his performance.

"Good," Suca commented. "Again!—My roon of min me say kay!"

Adrian sang along. "Come on, Doblin, let's get this vehicle moving!"

Doblin gave him a smug glance and soon joined in. The air filled with rich harmony, and Suca taught his friends the longer version. Adrian felt the vibration coming up through his body; the trunk purred like a kitten, then slid parallel to the small hill. Doblin struggled to steer the awkward contraption by grasping at the handle that was down on the side and shifting his body weight. Cree-L held tightly to Adrian's shirt, his tiny voice echoing with the rest. Adrian smiled in delight at the enchantment of the moment.

The trunk traveled smoothly up and over the small hill, leaving the vast Kinmont Mountains far behind. It sailed over the hard land surface with great ease, and then shimmied and bounced in time with the small quartet's appalling, inept voices. Adrian's legs grew numb from the constant rattling and shaking; the sensation of thousands of tiny quills poking his flesh, covered his throbbing legs. His voice quivered in reaction to the trunk pulsating over the sleek bumps and bounding around the slight curves.

At that moment, an unusual tremble shivered its way through the trunk from back to front. Adrian looked at his friends and could tell that they had sensed it too. He lifted his voice to its peak range and glanced curiously around the passing artificial land.

Thousands upon thousands of Simmels enclosed upon them, riding thin, silver-colored vibration boards. Adrian smiled at Suca. This was just the strong force he needed—the fulfillment of his journey had truly begun.

15
The Land of Puppets

The Simmels soon encircled them. Ahead, through the blue and green hues that reflected from the sky, appeared the outline of a large ship. Nary a person or creature stopped singing. The trunk bounced along with no signs of slowing and broke through the horizon, revealing the black loneliness of space. The land ended short of the great ship that had obviously been used as a docking bay.

Doblin, Suca, Adrian, and Cree-L immediately stopping singing and slowly brought the trunk to a rolling stop. Adrian looked back at the horizon that hey had just broken through. It appeared to be nothing more than a thick, colorful cloud; he then looked at the stars that twinkled above and jumped down off the trunk. The small group cautiously approached the massive ship, followed by a few of the very scared Simmels.

The ship, in some areas, had highlights of red, and upon a closer examination turned out to be millions of tiny men, no bigger than Adrian's pinky nail, wearing tiny, red jumpsuits and standing on intricate little scaffolds, while diligently repairing the outside of the ship. The vessel itself took on a very unique triangular state-of-the-art design, but appeared to be made out of nothing but rust and corroded metal.

"Ahoy down there!" A voice called out from the deck of the ship.

"Ahoy up there!" Adrian responded, not knowing what the correct response should be.

"Send a representative up to state your business!" the voice called again.

Adrian looked at Doblin and Suca. "I think I should go, I know the most about the mission."

"On the contrary, I should go," Doblin protested. "I have more knowledge about the planets and how to reach our destination."

Adrian gazed harder at Doblin. "Yes, but . . ."

Suca interrupted by calling back to the ship. "Can we send two representatives?!"

There was no answer. After a moment's pause, the voice yelled back, "Very well, but just two!" A long rope ladder suddenly flew over the side and rapidly unrolled down the side of the ship's exterior, stopping just above their heads.

Adrian walked to the edge of the pink plastic land and stared fearfully into the black infinity of space that loomed downward between the ship and the land. He gawked at the multiple stars far, far below and suddenly became totally overwhelmed. Doblin grabbed him by his shirt collar and boosted him to the last run of the ladder in one quick movement. He climbed the ladder with a quick burst of speed, flung himself over the top, then turned and helped Doblin.

A small, old man, no taller than Suca, carefully walked across the deck and stopped a cautious fifteen feet away. "Are you allies of foes?" he asked.

"We are friends," Adrian said.

"That is not what asked you! I want specifics!" the man said, sounding way too angry for Adrian's comfort.

"Sir, we are allies, sir!" Doblin cut in.

A smile crept across the old man's wrinkled face. He slowly grew to like Doblin and didn't know what to think about Adrian. "What is your business?" he asked.

Adrian stepped forward in another attempt to please the old man. "We seek the palace of King Adam."

"Call me *sir* when you address me!" the small man demanded.

Adrian backed up. He knew that if this old man were to meet Suca's reozzy, they would probably hit it off and spend hour after hour talking and planning his ultimate destruction. "Yes, sir," he moaned.

"That's better!" the old man grunted.

"Sir?" Doblin said, in his smooth metallic tone.

"Yes?"

"We seek transportation to the destination my comrade has just told you about."

The old man looked over the side of his ship. "I don't know, there are quite a few of you."

"Each man is supplied with and adequate amount of rations; the rest completely relies on your generosity, sir."

Cree-L continued to hide deep down in Adrian's pocket, listening intently to the going-ons outside, and had to keep himself from laughing hysterically as Doblin laid it on thick.

The old man turned to Doblin. "I can take you. I desperately need a crew this large to operate a ship as big as this one. Your Simmels will need training, of course, but we can work that out."

"Thank you, sir!"

"The only thing is . . ." the old man said, looking down at the floor of his ship. ". . . My final destination is the system of Tamane."

Doblin looked shocked. "Sir!" he yelled, then took a moment to calm down. "Sir, I beg your pardon, but that system is light years from where we need to be."

The old man stepped closer. "You need a ride and I need a crew, I don't see any other alternative for you." "Yes, sir What if we were to supply your ship with all the power we have and you supply us with just half a ride, say as far as the planet Trothlin?"

"That doesn't seem very reasonable on your part."

"I know, sir, but it is placed before you as an act of desperation."

The man turned away again. "Agreed," he said solemnly. "Have your Simmels board immediately, I'll lower the ramp." The little man walked away and disappeared into one of the ship's main rooms.

Over the side, Adrian watched as a main section of the ship's hull lowered like a drawbridge, revealing a cave-like entrance. The large exterior gate crashed down, smashing into the hard pink land and sending the Simmels bouncing around like helpless toys. Control was regained after a few hectic minutes, and Suca soon led his people on board.

The old man reappeared and explained how the old ship had once been a luxury cruise liner, then converted into a long-term battleship. He had purchased it some time ago before the previous owner had the chance to haul it off and recycle it into scrap metal. "I traded practically nothing for it," he explained. "Just a small amount of livestock." He then politely excused himself and busied himself the rest of the day, preparing the ship and making sure that his Simmel crew knew and understood how to operate the gigantic vessel.

Adrian didn't like the fact that he had to take half a day off from his utmost important journey. He tried to relax but couldn't. He gazed out into space and watched comets streak across the sky, something suddenly caught his eye, a giant destructive fireball surging upwards, tearing the very fabric of time and space; the substance of space peeled back and rolled like thin material, upsetting the surrounding stars and planets, causing each to jump from the ripple of their orbit and collide into each other. Adrian trembled in fear and disgust witnessing the lives of trillions vanquish abruptly without a trace.

Finally the moment of departure had arrived. The ship set out and sank beneath the pink land extension. Adrian looked up; the underneath side looked exactly the same as the top. It was a bewildering sight; the land jutted out of the clouds and fog that made up the atmosphere, with no visible means of support. The ship stopped and hovered, then proceeded with a very, very slow one hundred and eighty-degree turn.

The old man returned to the deck and led Adrian and Doblin into the small captain's quarters. He uttered a few quiet commands into his radio, and the ship commenced its long, slow, tedious expedition. Adrian was growing so anxious and restless that he could hardly contain himself. What could he do?—There was nothing he could do. He watched his hands shake. "Sir, can this ship go any faster?" he asked.

"We're full speed ahead now; it will just take time," the old man said calmly.

The calmness in his voice made Adrian relax, but he deeply rationalized the fact that they had ninety-six hours, or four days, left until the galaxy would be ripped apart and all the innocent would lose their lives. His hands began to sweat profusely.

Doblin took a seat in a small, hard chair. "Sir, who were those tiny men wearing the red jumpsuits we noticed working outside your ship?'

"They are called Shatenites. They have offered their services in exchange for transportation, much like yourself. I hired them to remove rust and repair minor holes and cracks that were forming on the outer hull. They did not get along with my last crew and chased them off. Fiesty people!"

"Sounds like my kind of people!" Cree-L said, looking up at Adrian.

"Shh!" Adrian returned.

"I was scared that they would not get along with your Simmels, but they seem to be getting along down there," the old man concluded.

Adrian, Doblin, and the old man engaged in conversation for many hours, while the ship slowly sauntered along. The old captain told Adrian of a possible method of growth: If he were to burrow himself deep into the giant cwalm seed and wait the period of one thousand years until the tree had reached maturity, he could break free and be three thousand times bigger than he was now. Adrian found this idea to be nothing more than a tall tale, but Cree-L was more than willing to try it.

Outside, the ravages of war continued, and drew nearer. Their meek transport continued to languish motionless in a subtle dead draw, until, the planet of Trothlin finally appeared in their path.

Out of nowhere, entry-ships quickly surrounded them and began transporting Adrian, Doblin, and the Simmels to the planet's surface. Doblin said a quick good-bye and departed with the rest. He gave one sorrowful glance back at the old ship and captain, lowered his head, and boarded the entry-ship with a small crowd of Simmels.

Adrian found it pleasant to be traveling on a faster ship to the planet Trothlin, even though he did not know his reason for being there, it was one small step forward. He arrived on the planet's surface shortly, stepped off the entry-ship into a blinding light that radiated down from the exotic blue electric sun above. Someone quickly shoved a pair of fuzz glasses into his hand, and he promptly put them on. He looked around at the beautiful new city in awe. Nothing was shaded like it would be if he was wearing a pair of traditional sunglasses—everything was bright and colorful. The city was full of life; androids clumsily tripped by carrying on with their own business, traveling this way and that, but there was something very unique and different about them at the same time. Each 'droid towed around a very small hovercraft that was attached to its back by a thin, single cable. In each small craft sat a tiny slug-like alien that controlled every movement the 'droid made. The 'droids were just a virtual mask—this was just a vast land of puppets. Adrian was very moved.

"Cree-L began to bellow from Adrian's shirt pocket. "I can't see! I'm blind," he cried.

Adrian motioned for one 'droid puppet to bring him a small pair of glasses. They had every shape and size. Cree-L tried on various sizes and colors until he found one that fit and looked just right.

"Thank you," Adrian said to the 'droid puppet. "I was wondering . . ." He stopped and moved to the other side of the 'droid so that he could talk directly to the alien. The small alien repeated the same avoidance process and jolted away. Adrian had enough and kindly gave in to the alien's game and awkwardly confided to the empty, shallow robot. "I was wondering if you had seen my friend Suca? I believe he was aboard another entry-ship that arrived earlier."

A deep robotic accent erupted from the thin robotic frame. "I know of no Suca."

Adrian looked around. "Are you sure there were no other ships that unloaded large groups of Simmels?"

"I know of no Suca," the robot repeated.

"How about Simmels? Have any of the ships brought any Simmels to port?"

"I know of no Suca," the robot again repeated.

Adrian tried to reason with the robot one last time in his own, best robotic accent. "Forget about Suca. Have the entry-ships brought Simmels to port?"

"Yes. As danger nears. All arrivals and residents must report to the rally."

"Where might this rally be?"

"I do not understand *might*."

Adrian remained calm. "Where is the rally location?"

"Straight ahead. left. straight ahead. left. right."

"Thank you."

"Do not understand . . ."

Adrian turned and ran before the 'droid could utter another word. He quickly found his friend Doblin, and the two men disappeared into the crowd following the 'droids directions. When they arrived at the outdoor arena where the rally was being held, they were surprised to see long lines that stretched for miles.

Adrian caught his breath. "We have no time for this. We need to find out what the current status of Diabolis is and keep going. Come on! We're going to have to cut in line!"

Doblin stood motionless.

"Come on!" Adrian repeated.

Doblin refused to move.

"Fine. You go find Suca, and afterward we'll meet right back here." He turned and made his way to the front of the line. Hefty security 'droids immediately stopped him in his track and pushed him stumbling back a couple steps.

"Back of the line," their voices clanked.

Adrian was not afraid of the giant 'droids because he truly knew what they were. He eyed the tiny creature that hovered in fear behind the mountainous robot. "Impressive 'droid you got here," he teased. "I wonder what would happen if I were to cut the lifeline you have attached to your friend here?!" he said, motioning to the 'droid. The aliens were weak; Adrian only needed to throw them off their guard long enough to duck inside.

The 'droids paused. Now was his chance. "Are you threatening us?" one said. By the time the words left his robotic lips, he looked down and Adrian was gone.

Adrian ran down the steps inside the packed arena and found a single empty seat halfway up from the small stage that had been built below. He squeezed down the row, past gawky 'droids that stared straight ahead with their lifeless metallic gazes. The alien controllers floated high above, extending their lifeline cables tightly, while vying for the best view of the going-ons.

Cree-L poked his head out of Adrian's pocket.

The stadium was filled with commotion; everybody was abuzz about what this mass meeting was about and how it would affect their lives.

Adrian looked down through the sea of aluminum heads and watched with interest, men like himself busying themselves in preparation for this most important event. A heavyset man approached the podium and requested the crowd to quiet down. Things did, and Adrian could feel the tension in the stadium grow. The man then explained to the assembled crowd that they had a very important speaker who had a message to share. The crowd began to softly mumble to each other, causing Adrian to miss the name of the important guest, but that was fine, he would find out who it was soon enough.

The man at the podium cracked a few corny off-the-wall jokes to loosen up the crowd, then introduced the guest speaker. Adrian's jaw dropped; he couldn't believe who he saw. His hands began to shake with excitement. He sat forward in his seat to get a double take just to be sure he wasn't seeing things. He tried to breathe deeply to help control his anxiety, but this time it wasn't working. There—just yards away from him—the one person he thought was dead-speaking to the crowd, was Rhesus! He had done it! Somehow, he had reached his dreams! He was speaking to the crowds of people he had always longed for. To extend his voice out and persuade the people to see everything that was true and righteous; to stand on their own feet and fight together for what they believed in.

"Beloved people of this beautiful land," Rhesus spoke, adjusting his awkward blue fuzz glasses. "My name is Rhesus Turnbuckle. I am on a journey in the name of King Adam to bring the people from both sides of the split galaxy together in one united front, to stand together against the evil that has been forced upon us from the evil Diabolis and his Die-cell warriors! We have been deceived! We the people must make the choice of our fate—and make it now! This glorious atom galaxy must not be divided! Our beloved king has left us with the opportunity to decide for ourselves how we wish to live and what path we wish to take? I have decided in my heart to seek your aid and ask you to stand together and defend our honor! Do you truly wish to live by Diabolis's plan?! I believe the answer is *No!* . . . We have never been a true unit in our mind and strength with each planet, city, and colony under individual government, to rule alone, and fend for ourselves! Diabolis has taken advantage of our weakness! He will unite us, but under his rule of pain and agony! Unite! Unite! Unite! Help your friends and neighbors! Let us maintain our freedom to govern ourselves as we wish! Do not let yourselves down! Join with me, now!"

The crowd seemed less than pleased and slowly trickled out of the arena one by one.

Rhesus then spoke to the one-third of the crowd that remained. "We have no time to waste," he continued. "We must leave on a very fierce attack right this very minute! I have received rumors that Diabolis is celebrating an early victory on Harmoroon-3! It is an intensely guarded planet, that is why I desperately seek your help! I have been spreading the word and have acquired a small army—so you will not be alone in your decision to battle!"

The crowd remained silent.

Rhesus clutched the podium tightly. "Come with me now! We will reconvene at the battle station, Movan!" He looked out over the crowd one last time, stepped away from the podium, and bounded off the small stage.

Adrian ran hard against the flow of the exiting crowd, leapt over the security barrier, through Rhesus's assembled entourage, and approached Rhesus. Rhesus was altogether shocked and pleased; he embraced Adrian without a care in the world.

"Forgive me!" Adrian begged.

"Forgive you for what?"

"For leaving you. I should have stayed and fought, rather than running like a coward."

"Don't be ridiculous. You had to run, it was the only way."

Adrian felt somewhat better. "I thought you were dead, how did you escape?"

"Diabolis just stunned us with some kind of radio micro-wave that temporarily crippled us. We woke up back in the cell and thought all was lost until the Varenetions attacked the Moon Probe and freed us."

"Yeah, I saw the attack from the planet Galla," Adrian said, adjusting his fuzz glasses.

Rhesus did the same and continued talking. "I made it out alive, but the Die-cells managed to get hold of Biggs. They better not do anything to him or I'll—"

"I know," Adrian interrupted, trying to keep Rhesus focused. "We need to go! You can fill me in with the rest of the details on the way,"

Rhesus's entourage gathered around them and escorted them out of the arena. Adrian felt like a dignitary.

16

Stormfront

Rhesus and Adrian met Doblin and Suca outside the arena, and after a brief introduction, they were off again.

Before long, they were standing outside the thick walls of the Movan battle station, where a tall, sleek alien was handing everybody who entered a small black device that resembled a television remote. Adrian looked casually down at the lightweight mechanism that fit snugly into the palm of his hand. The device featured two large buttons, one red and one green. Adrian continued inside while reading the small, white directions that were printed above the buttons: "Please press the red button first. After instructions are given, please press the green button. Thank you."

Adrian pressed the red button with his right thumb. A man's voice quietly sounded from within the device. "Greetings!" the voice said. "You are commando number 2-0-5-0. You will be issued: one laser gun, one full body suit of armor, and once cylinder space capsule. After you have assumed these items, please press the green button, thank you."

Rhesus, Doblin, and Suca listened to their hand-held devices in turn, which stated pretty much the same thing. The four men then walked over to the long table of gear and received their supplies. The assistants fitted Cree-L with his own personalized gear, while others rolled out the large cylinder space capsule. The capsule could hold five men comfortably. Since Doblin, Suca, Rhesus, and Adrian were lined up together at the door, and their numbers coincided—2050, 2051, 2052, 2053. This would ensure that they would ride together in the same capsule. Cree-L would continue to ride in Adrian's pocket, so the men met their fifth party member, Trog, who would have to sit in to conserve room in other capsules.

The six men found a quiet corner in the crowded battle station and pulled their black suits of armor over their clothes. To Adrian, the suit looked like a diver's wet suit, but at this point, he could not be picky. He left the front of his suit partially unzipped and returned Cree-L to his pocket.

After making sure everything was secure on his person, Adrian pressed the green button and listened to the same male's voice cut through the air: "Greetings! You have been assigned to an assault mission on Harmoroon-4. Your mission will consist of Die-cell depletion and the rescuing of allied comrades. You commander will be De-van-mine, who will meet you at the point of impact on Harmoroon-4. Any further questions should be directed to your superior officers. Die-cell warriors are estimated to be around five hundred in your designated point. Good luck on you mission, soldier—and thank you for using Delivunn portable communication systems!"

Suca listened in and scratched his fuzzy little head. "Me no understand the 'point of impact' part?"

"You will soon enough," Rhesus said. "Come on, let's roll!"

The five men rolled the pearl-like capsule to the nearest of the two hundred space shoots and stopped at the end of a long line. Assistants gathered up the small communication systems and fuzz glasses then opened an almost invisible door on the capsule.

Adrian was very excited and nervous. He swallowed hard, trying to subdue the tension, but it offered little relief.

One by one, the capsules shot up through the shoots like bullets firing from a gun, and soon it was their turn. The crew double-checked their harnesses that secured them to the somewhat soft seats and gave the outside assistants the thumbs-up when all was ready. The assistants closed and sealed the large hatch and rolled the capsule to the shoot. Inside everything remained steady and level. Adrian gritted his teeth and triple-checked his harness.

The capsule surged through the shoot, and before any of the passengers had time to realize, the capsule had exploded out into space.

"Wow! Can we do that again?!" Cree-L exclaimed.

"Maybe sometime," Adrian responded.

"Aren't these capsules fascinating?" Rhesus spoke up. "They manipulate time and space. They ride the ripples of space as if it were a small planet. Of course, Diabolis has caused so much commotion in the galaxy that we pretty much have to surf our way to Harmoroon-4."

Adrian could barely make out the planets and stars they passed, through the cloudy, outer shell of the capsule. He could feel the bouncing and jolting of the cylinder over each wave. He felt like a helpless beach ball, rocking back and forth out on the ocean.

"Look over there," Rhesus said, pointing. "I recognize those stars! The one on the far left in NuTron, and other on the right is ProTron."

"I recognize them as well," Doblin honed in.

For some reason those names sounded remarkably familiar to Adrian, but he just couldn't place them. He looked through the cylinder at the two stars. NuTron glowed a vibrant green, as opposed to ProTron's subtle pinks and reds. The two suns moved quickly out into space, obviously upset by the unsettling waves of Diabolis's fury.

Adrian sat back. Things grew quiet for some time. "Whatever happened to your reozzy? Did you finally get the gumption to put the thing down?" he asked Suca jokingly.

"No, he back at Trothlin with friends who no choose to fight."

Adrian was very relieved. He desperately hoped he would never see another reozzy as long as he lived. Adrian's thoughts were cut off when the capsule dipped suddenly straight down, in a terrible thrash of turbulence.

"Were getting too close to the tear in space!" Rhesus shouted. "Everybody undo your harness and stand in the middle!" he ordered.

"No! Too dangerous!" Suca squealed. He remained in his harness and watched the others assemble in the center.

"Okay, now run to that wall!" Rhesus yelled, over the deafening noise of space being ripped apart outside.

The crew stumbled across the cylinder and pressed against the wall with as much force as they could apply.

"Again!" Rhesus commanded.

The crew tried again, with overwhelming results. The capsule rolled up and over one ripple after another and came to rest in a snug-fitting dip.

"One more!" Doblin suggested.

The crew, again, poured the capsule over a few more high ripples, then paused to rest. Everything outside the capsule unemotionally began to quiet down.

"I believe we are on course now," Rhesus said, strapping himself back into his seat. "When we reach Harmoroon-4, we will circle it once and come in on the perihelion, got it?!"

"Same method?" Adrian asked.

"Same method," Rhesus confirmed.

"Can the Die-cells pick up the incoming space capsules on their radar?" Doblin asked.

"No, they are far too small. If by some chance they can, though, the radar will just bounce off the small circular frame and report a meteor shower."

Millions of pearl-like capsules continued to be dispatched from the battle station and streaked across space, pelting all fifteen known Harmoroon planets with a force that was unmatched by Diabolis himself.

The thousands of capsules designated for Harmoroon-4 joined in with the rotation around the unsuspecting planet and plummeted to the ground. Adrian held on tight to his seat as the capsule picked up speed. He watched the other capsules speed ahead through the almost-clear walls. He couldn't control his reaction to the moment and screamed a blood-curdling scream, as did the others.

"Hold on!" Rhesus yelled. "We cannot slow down! We have to take the Die-cells by surprise!"

The large pearl raced from the sky and splashed into a small lake, sending large walls of water crashing to the shore. Adrian was briefly disillusioned and quickly came to. He found himself under water and briefly wondered what had happened to the capsule and his friends. He swam briskly to the surface and hurriedly checked his pocket to console himself that Cree-L was still there—he was. His large fingers embraced Cree-L's face gently. Cree-L reached his tiny hand upward and patted Adrian's index finger as a sign that all was clear.

The capsule had disintegrated upon impact. Adrian looked around and noticed his friends swimming rapidly to shore. "Hold your breath," he told Cree-L and began swinging his arms in long beautiful strokes until he reached the water's edge. He pulled himself up onto the marshy land just as the lake swallowed a couple of more incoming pearl capsules.

Within minutes warfare guerrillas stormed out of the jungle along with commander De-van-mine. Without saying a word, they patiently checked behind every tree and disappeared back into the dark foliage. Adrian knew he had to be quick on his feet with this crowd or he would certainly perish. He met up with his friends and followed the soldiers into the jungle, keeping the sounds of their movement to a minimum. Adrian's eyes adjusted to the darkness. He could barely make out and avoid obstacles on the ground and low-lying branches; his ears focused on any sounds beyond those of the strange creatures that inhabited the jungle and listened for any signs of possible Die-cell activity.

Hushed whispers beyond the row of hardwood trees made the troop stop for a moment. De-van-mine couldn't make out the words but he reasoned that there had to be more than twenty Die-cells beyond.

The ambush was on.

De-van-mine's troops flowed from the shelter of the trees like wild men. Ramming their guns against their shoulders, they fired fiercely, unleashing a torrent of death.

Rhesus ran back to Adrian, "It's our job to enforce an attack on the prison camps ourselves, come on!"

Adrian placed his left hand on Rhesus's back so he could follow closely, while keeping his eyes and ears alert to the gunfire and Die-cell warriors that were all about them. He pulled out his gun and fired at random, dearly wishing that he had more training. A shot suddenly pounded against his chest just inches to the right of his unzipped armor, leaving a large gaping hole. He rapidly checked to see that he was okay, then mentally traced the trajectory of the blast back to two lone Die-cells standing on the roof of one of the prison houses. With a quick burst of speed he fired, knocking both men from the roof to the ground.

Other aliens, that had arrived late in their space capsules, advanced from the rear to aid in the ambush. They stormed over the ramparts, firing, shouting, and blasting, until every last Die-cell lay lifeless among the mounds of dirt. They streamed into the prison houses, tearing down doors and sections of walls.

The Die-cells retreated.

Adrian looked back at the hundreds of aliens that remained outside and followed Rhesus through the crowded, dirty prison house. The prisoners were packed in like sardines and pressed forward to the open door.

"Biggs!" Rhesus yelled.

"Are you looking for Seth Biggs?" a weak voice huffed.

"Yes," Rhesus replied, looking down at a small prisoner who was still bound by chains.

"He is in the next facility over."

"Thank you," Rhesus said, graciously. He motioned to an alien comrade to come over and remove the pale creature's heavy chains, then turned and ran out of the door, with the fleeing prisoners and Adrian close behind.

Pearl capsules assaulted the medium-sized Harmoroon orb with the aggression of ants pouring over a savory sugar cube that landed near their mound, until the prison camps had just about been vacated. Transport ships arrived late and had swiftly begun to transport women and children back to their home planets, while able-bodied men were encouraged to recoup and stay and fight.

Rhesus ran, grabbed the edge of the door, and swung himself into the next prison house. "Biggs!"

Adrian rounded the corner and saw Rhesus standing motionless. Two alien comrades approached from the corner, helping along a skinny, limping, undernourished—Seth Biggs.

"Biggs!" Rhesus yelled again.

Seth pushed his hat back and squinted at the duo. "Hi, guys," he said, then passed out.

Several alien comrades rushed over to revive him. "We need to get him out of here," one said.

"Follow me," Rhesus said. "Commander De-van-mine has supplies."

The aliens scooped Seth up and carried him out the doors, over the harsh, rough ground, while Adrian took up the rear. There were no signs of Die-cells anywhere. But they had to be there, possibly lurking in the trees. Their retreat had been inevitable, but still way too easy.

They soon reached Commander De-van-mine's temporary headquarters, which was located in a small clearing, complete with five large camouflage tents that had been erected earlier that day. They were very surprised to find the commander lying down in his tent—wounded. Medical personnel ran from his side and rapidly attended to Seth.

Rhesus picked up his friend's thin arm. "He was fine a minute ago, just very weak."

The medical assistant looked into Rhesus's eyes. "We'll take care of him, but the commander would like to see you."

Adrian could clearly see that Rhesus had reached a high status. The other prisoners were to be revived and transported, fifty miles to the east, and not anywhere near the headquarters, or the likes of a commander and his specialized medical doctors.

Rhesus laid Seth's thin arm down and slowly walked to the tent. He threw the camouflage flaps back and ducked inside.

"Rhesus?" De-van-mine moaned. He had his uniform ripped open to expose the bandages that covered a massive wound that ran down the middle of his torso and a large bandage around his right leg.

"Yes."

"Come closer."

Rhesus took a few small steps. "What happened?"

"That's not important," the commander choked. "The Die-cells are still out there. Our lookout satellite has reported no ships have left Harmoroon-4 since three rotations ago. I received word that the last count of Die-cell casualties stood at about four million, that's about half the expected population."

"I'll rally the troops again—we'll fight harder."

"No, that's not want I want from you."

"What do you want, sir?"

"I . . . I want you to leave."

"Leave, sir? Why?"

"Our comrades on Harmoroon-3 are not faring as well. They have been cut to thirty-five percent. I want you to gather your men, take one of our ships, and attack Diabolis personally."

"But, sir, I have no battle expertise."

"You have vision. You have spent so much time and energy spreading the word for people to get up and do something—it is only right that you should take out the evil."

"But, sir . . ."

"Was it not you who said: 'If every man gave something small to everybody he met, every man would receive a surplus of everything he needed that would exceed his wildest imagination.'"

"Yes, sir, I recall saying that."

"Good! Go forth and rely on your vision. I will supply you with my best ship and a few strategic soldiers who have been trained on land, sea, and air. Gather the four or five men you see fit and depart at once. My men and ship are one mile directly to the north. We believe Diabolis's coordinates to be at 9753—tell nobody that until it is absolutely necessary."

"Sir, I . . ." Rhesus paused. ". . . I thank you."

De-van-mine smiled.

Rhesus bowed politely and ran from the tent. He reached the medical doctors and found that Seth had regained consciousness, but he would not be able to accompany him on his mission. He gathered Adrian, Doblin, and Suca—and with a heart filled with vengeance, he led the three men into the shadow of the jungle.

17

Nocturnal Riots

Rhesus stood back from the ship's steering controls. "Any sign of Harmoroon-3?" he asked, trying to sound official. He was but a humble student in his mind, and yet, the five soldiers who sat before him were under his command. They could run through any tactical maneuver in their sleep, but they had also been taught extreme discipline and would happily play along—at least for the time being.

"All scanners are dry, sir," one soldier spoke up.

"Good," Rhesus replied.

"Estimated time of arrival is .121!"

"Steady on course," Rhesus commanded.

"Suggestion, sir?" another soldier said.

"Yes?"

"Suggest we reduce speed and continue cautiously—we are in a war zone, sir."

Rhesus felt a little embarrassed. "Okay," he said. "What is your name soldier?"

"Gunner, sir."

"Excellent, Gunner, I'm leaving you in charge of tactical maneuvers on our mission."

"Request to ask your permission before any maneuver is attempted."

Rhesus smiled. "So be it."

Suddenly, a silent alarm activated on the dash. "Sir, we've got a problem," a third soldier spoke up.

"What is it?"

"It appears that the Die-cells have formed a blockade."

Gunner turned to Rhesus. "Request permission to maneuver," he said.

Rhesus smiled again. "Granted."

Gunner sped the ship to full throttle and raced to the blockade. The Die-cells abruptly fired on impulse at the motion of Gunner's ship, as he looped through each passing blaze. Gunner did not fire in return; he continued to dip and weave through the Die-cell ships like a madman. The Die-cells held formation and intensified their fire power one fold.

Gunner figured he could outstrip them; he ran circles around each ship in turn, barely avoiding several powerful blows. The Die-cells buffeted each other violently, causing one or two to explode into a destructive end.

"That will show them!" Gunner exulted. He straightened out the ship and advanced without varying speed to the nearby unseen planet of darkness and evil.

"Harmoroon-3 straight ahead, sir, and approaching rapidly."

"Yes, I can see it from here, but . . ." Rhesus said, then stopped. "That can't be it." He looked out into a flat wasteland of sand."

Gunner flew over the desert, creating a sandstorm that pulled up into the thruster's shockwave, stirring up a dust-devil that chased them for many miles.

"I'm going to have to land, sir," Gunner said.

Rhesus took a minute to think. "Yes, you're right—go ahead and land."

"Thank you, sir." Gunner reduced speed, banked the ship slightly to the left to avoid the dust-devil, hovered briefly—then landed. He then cut most of the auxiliary power, leaving the craft to run idle. He had learned, a few years ago, to never shut the power off completely unless it was absolutely necessary. That was back when some space bandits had tried to mug him—and that was something that would never happen again.

The small crew waited momentarily until the dust-devil had passed completely, then stepped out of the ship.

"Are you sure this is Harmoroon-3?" Rhesus asked, looking across the sculptured, wind-blown sand hills.

"Positive," the lowest-ranking soldier spoke.

"Well, we can go back over the computer's readings," Gunner suggested.

"Go ahead, I'll wait out here," Rhesus said, still transfixed on the golden sand.

Just then, the sky grew dark, and the wind grew cold. Clouds tumbled toward them as the wind blew harder. It appeared to Adrian like a film trick Braddock had once shown him called, 'time-lapse photography'. The sky then split open and poured rain. Adrian turned his face downward from the storm and tried to run back to the shelter of the ship, but it was no use. The wet sand clung to his boots and pulled him down, down, until it reached his knees. The other men fought back ferociously, but they only sank faster.

"Hold still!" Rhesus shouted, through the thundering rain.

Minutes later, the men were completely engulfed and pulled down into the depths of the sand. Still struggling, they broke through the other side below and into the dark, black weightlessness of space.

Adrian couldn't even see the fingers that he held just inches from his face. It was so dark. He stretched his arms out as far as they could extend, but he felt nothing; he kicked his legs rapidly to slow his rate of descent, but couldn't sense if he was falling. As far as he was concerned, he was in a state of suspended animation. He listened, but heard nothing; he thought but could think nothing. He cried out, but couldn't hear his own voice . . . then—his right foot—something sturdy was supporting his right foot. He tapped his toes with anticipation. He heard a giant, hollow thud that vibrated through his body as his recollection slowly seeped back. Both feet settled on the object and Adrian cringed downward, feeling the rough surface with his hands. The picture that came to his mind from the object was very familiar—but he couldn't place it.

"Can anybody hear me?" a familiar voice rang out.

It was Suca.

"Yes!" Adrian yelled.

"Adrian! Adrian, is that you?"

"Yes," Adrian yelled back.

"Where are we?" Suca panicked.

Adrian peered into the darkness, only to see nothing but black. Had he gone blind? He didn't know.

"Me've gone blind!" Suca screamed.

Adrian suddenly felt relief run through his body. He hadn't gone blind!

"No, you haven't gone blind," another voice said, settling onto the mysterious object.

Adrian could recognize Doblin's voice anywhere.

". . . It is only darkness, Doblin continued.

"Diabolis's darkness," Rhesus added, as the rest of the crew settled onto the top of the ship.

Below, the lights of a distant city took shape and illuminated the silhouette of the object on which they stood. Adrian couldn't believe it—the small crew was standing on top of the ship and gently descending toward the city.

"How is this possible?" Adrian asked. "Who is controlling the ship?"

"Nobody," Rhesus said, "we've hit a polarity stream. The pull downward is obviously slightly greater than the pull upward."

To Adrian, those were the words Braddock would have spoken. He smiled contentedly and sat back against the ship, while leisurely checking on Cree-L.

The ship proceeded down, and with each drop in altitude, things around them grew fiercer. Bombs blasted into the sturdy high-rises; lights blinked and flashed within the buildings; people ran and screamed in the streets, turning over small land crafts and blasting projectile weapons into mobs of people and Die-cell soldiers. People had gone crazy and were destroying everything in sight, including comrade aliens.

Adrian watched the commotion until he grew sick. He turned his head quickly to the shadowed buildings that stretched high above them as they continued to sink down. He let his mind stray into the night.

Gunner climbed over the ship's edge and leapt inside, revving the engines as they neared the street. He reached back around the ship's cap from the open hatch and pulled Rhesus inside, followed by Suca.

A blast suddenly erupted from above, causing a large portico to collapse and crash right beside them, killing several people below. The ship jumped and skidded through the air, dove down and scraped its belly along the pavement. Masses of wild people stampeded toward the helpless craft, hit it like a wall, crushing the front runners, and fiercely began to rock it from side to side.

Gunner's men instinctively leapt from the ship and pushed the crowd back, allowing Doblin and Adrian to scramble inside. Gunner slammed the throttle to full power and arched the ship up and over the terrified crowd.

"Close the hatch!" Rhesus yelled.

"What about Gunner's men?" Suca protested.

Rhesus turned to the small man. "They can help take care of the crowd! We won't need them where we're going!"

Gunner seemed disgruntled. "Where are we going?" he said, keeping the ship in a low hover.

"The coordinates are 9753!"

"Comeback on that?" Gunner said.

"Coordinates . . . 9753!"

"Sir, I've never heard of that, and the computer doesn't show any response."

"I know it exists! Just find a way to get us there, fast!"

"Okay, I'll see what I can do." Gunner revved the engines again and rocketed the ship skillfully through the buildings and high-rises, past the bombs that exploded all around; above the multicolored neon lights that ran along the street, and safely out of the fascinating nocturnal city.

Images calmly clouded Adrian's mind, blocking his surroundings and enveloping his soul with the fear of death. The end had come. All was lost. He collapsed to a sitting position against the wall and clawed at his hair, trying to remove the image—where was Braddock when he needed him!

"What be that up ahead?" Suca declared.

Adrian's hearts skipped a beat; his surroundings returned to his vision; his fingers grew icy and numb. He looked around fearfully and staggered to an upright position on his weak, trembling legs to see what Suca had pointed out.

"I don't know," Gunner said. "But it looks like that would be your 9753 coordinates."

Adrian began to relax. His breath slowly poured back into his lungs in thin bursts; he took a few moments to pause, then stared through the view shield at the strange tower that had everybody captivated.

The thin, gray, windowless tower stood alone—and rightly so. Thin billows of smoke circled the outer construction from the base and trickled upward in a condensed stream.

Rhesus noticed a dim flickering light shining from a small crevice in the building's lining. "There!" he pointed out.

"What are you orders, sir?" Gunner asked patiently.

"Attack," Adrian blurted out.

Rhesus turned to Adrian sternly, then smiled. "Yes," he said, "Attack."

The ship took off full speed toward the tower and advanced in an onrush straight for the small glimmer of light.

"Faster!" Rhesus ordered. "We're breaking through!"

Suca jumped. "No, we be not! You let me off here!"

Gunner singled his mind to the one task at hand. "This is as fast this baby can go. I'll have to melt the wind resistance!"

A heavy red light shot out from the front of the craft several feet, briefly burst into flames, then covered the ship with a bright red, resistant-slick glow. The pace of the ship quickly doubled, and soon tore through the light opening, destroying the entire wall, and slid across the slick floor of the inner room.

"We be dead!" Suca screamed.

The ship crawled to a slow stop and came to rest facing the damaged wall they had just collided through. Everybody aboard gathered their senses and clutched their guns tightly.

"We dead?" Suca mumbled.

"Of course not!" Doblin snapped, opening the hatch.

The men cautiously stepped out, scanned the room thoroughly, and marched on.

Rhesus noticed the room was remarkably similar to the room that he had encountered on the Moon Probe, which stirred his mind even more.

"I think I just saw something move," Adrian advised. "There . . . the shadows."

He was right. The shadows slid slowly down off the walls and slithered across the floor, causing the small crew to stumble backward in fear. The shadows rolled together in a tube, spun up into the air like a tornado—and out stepped Diabolis, swathed in a great cloak of black, armed with a very peculiar weapon. "You have been pursuing me, I hear, and pursue me no more you will," he roared. "Prepare to die!" He then clenched his designer gun and stepped to the side coldly.

The wind of the twister that swirled behind him howled like a scream, then vanished, though his cloak continued to blow in an unseen breeze.

A small troop of Die-cells appeared from behind and erupted onto the scene in a blaze of gunfire. Doblin and Gunner spun around and angrily returned fire. The Die-cells quickly retreated through a wall that had appeared solid, followed by Doblin, Suca, and Gunner. Things were definitely not what they seemed, so every man had to be on his guard.

Cree-L squirmed loose from Adrian's pocket, dropped to the floor, and quickly ran off.

"Come back!" Adrian called. But Cree-L had disappeared from sight.

Only Rhesus and Adrian remained to fight Diabolis.

"So, your friends desert you as this one did before," Diabolis said, pointing to Adrian.

Adrian bit his lip. "It will not happen again. I will not leave while you are still alive," he said, stepping forward.

"How very brave of you, but you will need better weapons," Diabolis spoke.

Adrian felt his gun pull from his hands and fly through the wall. He was completely dumbfounded—soon, another long silver gun appeared in his grip, and the walls vanished, revealing a series of rooms and long hallways. Adrian eyed the strange looking weapon over very quickly. The name of the gun, a Rike Air Palmer, was etched down the side of the barrel. What a cool name. But Adrian had to turn his attention back to Diabolis.

"Here, we play by my rules," Diabolis continued, turning and running down one of the many hallways."

"Great! Hide-and seek," Adrian said.

"Hide-and what? Rhesus asked.

"Never mind."

The duo dashed down the corridor that Diabolis had just fled down, met up with the evil being again, and fired their guns simultaneously. Small, colorful balls of compressed air blasted form the gun and exploded on either side of the evil man.

"Good move," Diabolis scoffed, firing two rounds of purple, yellow, and red balls of deadly air in quick succession.

Rhesus anticipated his move and darted to the right—Adrian to the left. The volley of air power hurled between them and crashed into the rear wall, allowing Diabolis time to escape into the next room.

Rhesus and Adrian followed, wasting no time. The surface of the floor was by far slicker than that of the last. Rhesus relaxed and skated across the room as graceful as a figure skater; he controlled his acrobatic moves, pulling off figure eights, spins, and attempted a back flip. He then flew past the distracted Diabolis, and with a quick movement, threw his cloak over his face. "Fire!" he yelled.

Adrian realized he was not in position, he was too caught up in Rhesus's stunts. He held his stance and ricocheted an orange blast off the wall that slammed indiscriminately under Diabolis's feet, knocking him to the ground.

Rhesus slid over to the cloak that lay in a bundle. "He's gone!" he shouted.

"That was easy," Adrian said in delight.

"No, I mean," he disappeared.

Adrian froze. He could sense that Diabolis was standing right behind him. "Rhesus!" he cried weakly.

Rhesus spun, firing a green blast directly at Adrian that barely fazed past his head. He quickly ducked and looked up just in time to see Diabolis run into another room.

"He's playing mind games," Rhesus pointed out. "Be careful."

Adrian had his fill. He charged into the next room, washing everything with a bath of blasts; one yellow ball bounded around and chopped into Diabolis" side. He yelled in agony and dropped to his knees, pounding multiple blasts where Adrian had been standing.

Rhesus cut to the other side of the room. Victory was about to be his. "It is over!" he yelled, keeping his gun aimed at his victim. "Your precious Harmoroon planets have been captured, and your Die-cells depleted. The people have spoken, and your rule is over! It is now my pleasure to bring and end to your reign of terror!"

Diabolis held his side and laughed. "Do you honestly believe that taking me down is that easy?" His eyes suddenly glowed bright red; his clothes bursts into flames, which radiated depression rather than heat; he slowly tripled in size, as the flames about him burned higher. He bared long white fangs and began to speak again. "Now! Behold my true wrath! You will die a slow, painful death filled with torture over the next one thousand years!!"

Rhesus fired a tri-burst at his adversary, then fled the room and ran back to the ship. Adrian followed, blasting his air gun back at Diabolis whenever he saw the chance.

The men were trapped. Their guns shorted out at Diabolis's command and the walls reappeared between them and Diabolis, confining them to one room once again.

Diabolis's mutated arms and ripped through the wall, spewing his evil presence into the room; he glared at Adrian and Rhesus face to face. "Die!" he moaned, growing larger still.

Rhesus and Adrian held their breath as Diabolis extended his arms.

At that moment, a small series of muffled explosions rumbled from beneath the ship. A bright light suddenly filled the room as an extreme lightning blast belted from the ship's guns and slammed into Diabolis, knocking him back through the wall.

"Who fired that blast?" Adrian yelled.

"Get back in the ship!" a voice called urgently.

Adrian turned—it was Gunner, leaping out of the holographic wall from the other side of the room. "Get back in the ship! Now!" he yelled, leaping into the shelter of the craft.

Doblin leapt out of the wall next, carrying Suca. He ran to the hatch and tossed his little friend inside.

Diabolis viciously yelled from the next chamber.

"He's coming back!" Rhesus cried.

"We've got to leave, now!" Adrian begged.

"No! Leave me! I will finish Diabolis alone! Go!" Rhesus pleaded.

Doblin shifted his weight from the open hatch, stomped over, and picked Rhesus up off the ground effortlessly.

"NO!" Rhesus screamed, like one of the million helpless people who had lost their freedoms and had been dragged away from their families and loved ones, only to find themselves being held captive at one of the prison camps. ""Let me go! This is my destiny! Let me go!"

Suddenly, Diabolis tore back through the wall, his eyes glowing as bright red as ever. He had grown nine times his size; evil poured from every pore of his body; he howled like one thousand blood-thirsty wolves, then tore toward the ship in a full-blown run.

Adrian gasped, then ran to the ship with everything he had. He helped Doblin stuff Rhesus deeper into the ship, then slammed the outer hatch door closed.

Another pulsing light of extreme fire blasted from the ship, momentarily diverting Diabolis's furry for another few precious seconds.

Adrian turned and looked at the console—it was Cree-L.

"Fire! Again! Again!" Rhesus continued to yell. "We can't let him get away! FIRE! FIRE! FIRRRRE!!"

The floor suddenly began to lean; the ship slid into the outer wall of the room and stopped. Gunner pounded switches and levers on the control panel, firing the boosters.

"Shoot him! Shoot him! You don't know what you're doing!! Shoot him!!"

Gunner lifted the craft off the ground and exploded out of the aperture.

"Shoot him!" Rhesus continued to scream hopelessly.

Gunner guided the ship as far as he could and spun back around to face the tower. To everyone's amazement, the tower rocked back and forth, then in a rush of power, blasted off from the ground and exploded into space like a rocket ship, ripping through the sandy outer layer.

Rhesus briefly seemed to regain control. "Follow him!" he ordered.

"Yes, sir," Gunner replied. He throttled the boosters to maximum and took off after the vanishing tower-ship.

"Where are they?" Adrian asked.

"Straight ahead! But, that's bizarre," Gunner said.

"What?" Suca questioned.

"They are feinting to the right."

"What is so bizarre about that?" Doblin asked.

"That maneuver, it's just . . . ."

Suddenly, the entire crew grew silent and stared in disbelief out of the front view shield.

"The Moon Probe!" Rhesus stammered.

The crew sat motionless and watched the tower-ship enter the giant orb through the south pole. Any hope of catching up was suddenly dashed.

Rhesus walked to the back of the ship with his head hung low. His mission was over. Diabolis only needed but a few more moves—and the game was his.

He . . . he had won . . .

18

Atom

The small ship and crew drifted through space in no particular direction, bouncing off space rubble from destroyed planets and sailing through misty gases.

"Where we be going?" Suca subtly asked.

"Does it really matter?" Rhesus quipped.

Adrian sat quietly at the console next to Gunner, who was slouched back with his eyes closed. He watched numbingly out of the view screens at the passing planets that circled around them in disarray, while his mind drifted back to Braddock.

The black planet of Mylin flew by in the storm. Its thick, black crust torn apart by red and orange lava that now seeped out through new cracks, creating massive continents. Consword, the larger yellow slick surface planet, raced by next, following Mylin.

Adrian took special notice of the planet Sizab, a blue holographic orb that had once been negatively charged. But the most beautiful planet of them all, which soared up from below, was the crystal orb of Meeyanmay, which collided and smashed into the asteroid z-zone-6, causing the gorgeous, fragile, crystal ball to shatter into trillions of glass splinters shortly after it appeared into view.

The entire crew watched the destruction, showing no emotion, until a single, white pillar of light cut through the surrounding doom, highlighted by the space dust, and befell the entire ship. Each man's soul suddenly stirred, and each knew the light shining from ahead was meant specifically for him.

Adrian sat transfixed, as if in a dream, and sat back comfortably, watching the white light draw them in safely through the destructing space rocks and asteroids until they found themselves in the very eye of the storm.

Rhesus's gaze followed the beam of light to the source. "That's . . . that's King Adam's castle," he stuttered.

Every man remained calm and joyous as if he had been sitting they're staring at the castle for a thousand years. The peace they felt was not overwhelming, this was where they belonged, and this was where they longed to be.

They marveled in speechless wonder at the white spear-like towers that sat magnificently upon the giant red and white molecule base that suspended itself in space.

Gunner reverently jetted the ship once around the holy towers for a better look, then piloted the craft down from behind, through the large red and white molecules, until he had flown the craft completely underneath the castle and located a decent docking site at one of the many green stems that connected several molecules at the base outside the front gate.

Adrian and Suca were the first to unboard. They stepped out onto the curved surface of the stem and gasped at the beauty. Soon all was unloaded, and the small crew began their journey up, around, and over many molecules until they reached the large front door.

Doblin approached the large brass knocker that had been carved into a strange yet majestic creature that dwarfed him in size. He took hold of the heavy brass ring that the creature clenched tightly between his teeth, lifted it with both hands, and let it drop one time.

The team then listened as the loud signal of their presence echoed throughout the chamber within. The large door swung silently open.

"Is anybody home?" Cree-L bellowed from Adrian's pocket.

Adrian was not quick to silence his little friend, instead he walked proudly on, admiring the dark, finely crafted wood floors that were outlined with thick red carpet. The walls were artfully covered with a strange tan material that had been etched with scenes of former battles, and all around stood statues, lusciously draped curtains with tassels, and high, pointed ceilings with beautiful colorful murals.

At the center of the room sat the back of a mighty throne atop three silver circular landings, the widest at the base, and the smallest at the top. The bottommost landing slowly began to rotate clockwise, then clicked with some unseen gears, catching the second, then the third, until all three had rotated one full turn. The mighty throne then followed—and sitting there humbly was the almighty King Adam.

The small crew dropped to their knees in humility.

All three silver landing swallowed each other until the mighty throne sat on ground level.

"Please rise," the King's voice calmly commanded, "for it is I who should commend you."

Adrian raised his head in great admiration, then examined every last stitch of the King's majestic wardrobe. He wore no crown over his dark brown hair that Adrian had once imagined, but only sported velvet robes and a long flowing cloak.

"We failed, master," Rhesus said, returning to his feet.

The mighty King rubbed his chin profoundly, sat forward in his throne, and looked directly into Rhesus's eyes. "When people unite—we are as one. When people elect a king—it is one man, and that man must obtain corruption to maintain power—I do this not!"

"You are a noble king, sire," Rhesus said.

The King then turned his attention to every individual man in the party and continued. "You *are* very brave. Sailing on a smooth galaxy never made a skilled fighter pilot."

All present sat in bewilderment at the wisdom of those words.

Cree-L rolled his eyes, he was not so convinced.

"Excuse me!" Cree-L shouted, leaping from Adrian's pocket.

Adrian fell to the floor in an attempt to catch the little man who was now running toward the King, but Cree-L eluded his large fingers.

Cree-L stopped at his Majesty's feet and looked up "Sire, I don't know what you are talking about, but your evil counterpart, Diabolis, has escaped into the Moon Probe and we seek your help."

King Adam chuckled, picked Cree-L up, and set him on his lap. "All will be fine," he said.

"Begging your pardon, sire," Rhesus intruded, "but though we've captured fourteen of the Harmoroon planets, and the fifteenth is sure to follow, I feel that we have lost."

"Sire, I guess we were hoping to find great armies to conquer the Moon Probe, but your castle seems to be vacant," Adrian added.

Rhesus nodded in agreement.

King Adam stood. "Oh, but it is not empty. I want you to meet my daughters, Stasia and Odette," he said, returning Cree-L to the ground.

"Your Majesty, this is a matter of urgency!" Rhesus begged, heedlessly.

King Adam's two lovely daughters entered in from across the room and glided wistfully across the floor, wearing long, flowing, magnificent royal green gowns.

The two sisters stopped at their father's side, smiled politely, and maintained their royal dignified posture. Stasia's blond, golden hair hung down loosely at shoulder length; a stunningly beautiful contrast to her full, bright red lips. Odette's thick black hair was as dark as the night sky, and with it pulled up and artfully laced with flowers on top of her head, her beautiful, flawless blue skin shown radiantly.

Never in Adrian's short life had he ever seen a young lady as lovely as Stasia. He tried desperately not to stare, but he couldn't help it; his eyes flicked back and forth between King Adam and his lovely daughter.

Stasia tilted her head slightly to one side and briefly smiled at him, then returned her crystal-clear blue eyes back in the direction of her father.

Adrian's heart began to pound, his knees suddenly became weak. He had never experienced this sensation before. Was he coming down with some strange illness? No, he was far too happy. He turned his head to look at his friends, but his gaze returned to Stasia like a magnet. He could hear his Majesty speaking, but he couldn't make out the words. He hoped that Stasia would turn and look at him again, to give him another sign that she liked him, or was she just playing with his emotions? Maybe she didn't like him at all! Yes, that was it. He couldn't analyze it anymore, he had to concentrate.

"It is time," the mighty King said.

"For what?" Suca asked.

"For the beginning.

"Beginning of what?" Adrian questioned, returning Cree-L to his shirt pocket.

The King motioned toward two, ten-foot glass doors that stood across the room about where Stasia had appeared from. "If you'll just escort your party out onto my balcony, you will see."

The small group did as they were told, their heavy feet clomping along, echoing through the hallowed grandeur hall, through the large glass doors, and out onto the splendid balcony.

They waited.

"What we supposed to look for?" Suca asked impatiently.

The King remained silent.

Adrian looked out over the balcony's edge into the thick space dust that seemed to be slowly drifting away. His attention was suddenly distracted from a movement to his right; he turned eagerly. Stasia swayed nonchalantly, stepped over and stood beside him, and looked out into space as well. His symptoms started again. He had to be brave. Out of nervousness he reached down and took her hand.

Stasia turned to him with a straight face, then released her beautiful smile. Adrian smiled in return, and together they gazed longingly out into deep space.

"Look! It's the Moon Probe!" Suca pointed out.

The space dust cleared, exposing the vulnerable Moon Probe on the vast black sea of destruction that it had created.

At that moment, a strong, heavy wind surged over the castle. The mighty structure then began to vibrate with powerful sporadic convulsions, sending Adrian and Stasia tripping back to the castle walls for something to hold onto.

The building was out of control—Adrian felt dizzy. But with one resilient burst, the storm was over.

Everyone sat up, Adrian found that he had bounced dangerously close to the balcony's edge. He rose slowly and looked out over the short wall that separated him from infinity. He couldn't believe his eyes.

The sky was filled with thick, tangled gray and brown hair. One giant red eye with streaks of yellow, and a large black pupil, peered out through the fur and looked down on them.

"What is that?" Rhesus asked in complete amazement.

King Adam had been the only man standing through the ordeal. "That my friends, is an Aviv-Trenine."

Nobody in the history of the Atom Galaxy had ever seen a beast that enormous and powerful. Until now, they had been oblivious to the fact that there were larger worlds, much like Braddock had been too smaller ones. King Adam had known the truth all along and utilized their power. He was truly the man to be King.

Suddenly to everyone's amazement, the huge beast extended his long neck and swallowed the Moon Probe whole.

King Adam was right; the beginning had arrived.

Diabolis was gone.

19

The Final Game

The shocked, but relieved group, returned to King Adam's main chamber for a short victory party. Food and drinks were ushered in by well dressed servants and everybody began to cheer, but Adrian could tell that something was still not right with the King. The King began to pace back and forth in front of his throne, then stopped.

"Adrian? May I have a word with you?" he called out nervously.

Adrian approached and bowed politely. "Yes, your Majesty?"

"Follow me, please."

Adrian did as he was instructed and followed the King across the main chamber and into a small room off to the side. The room contained only one small wooden table, seven chairs, and was about as big as Adrian's bedroom back home.

King Adam closed the door behind them and instructed Adrian to sit down, then took a seat himself.

"Yes, sire? What did you want to see me about?" Adrian asked politely.

The King looked Adrian directly in the eyes. "Do you have any questions for me?" he asked.

Adrian was taken aback. "No."

"Are you sure?"

"I'm pretty sure." Then Adrian paused. "Well, other than going home, I did wonder a time or two during this adventure if my friends and I were supposed to destroy Diabolis, or if you were supposed to. But it looks as if you were the promised one all along."

King Adam chuckled. "I was only one-third of the plan. Rhesus was one-third, and now you are the final third."

"Me, sire?"

"Yes. Rhesus developed the coalition that destroyed most of the Die-cells and freed the slaves. I summoned the Aviv-Trenine that destroyed the Moon Probe and Diabolis's body. And you will . . ."

"What do you mean, 'Diabolis's body'?" Adrian interrupted.

King Adam stared harder. "Diabolis lives and you will finish him off!"

"What? You can't possibly mean that!"

King Adam sat back in his chair to ease some of the sudden tension in the room. "Do you know what the Circle of Simplicity is?" he asked softly.

Adrian had no idea and didn't respond, but a look of concern must have appeared on his face because King Adam continued with an explanation.

"The Circle of Simplicity is like a giant circle, a paradox, an oxymoron if you will. In a lot of ways it contradicts itself. For example, when we first invented the hovercraft, it was sluggish and couldn't move very fast. It could only levitate a few inches from the ground and was made of very, very heavy metal and other materials. But now days it is made very inexpensive, paper thin, and can go at unheard of rates of speed, because it went full circle in the Circle of Simplicity! If it's technology were to advance, it would appear seemingly more worthless and fragile, but would be far more powerful and efficient. The human body is the most advanced creation of all time! It's brain is faster than any computer, it's body is more agile than any ship, but it's the most fragile thing in the galaxy, and we use it to build inexpensive hovercrafts and other seemingly worthless devices that don't perform to the equality of our bodies—because it went full circle in the Circle of Simplicity! C.O.S., as we like to call it.

Adrian took it in for a minute but was still confused.

"I am saying that you are here for a reason," King Adam continued. "We, with our mortal bodies, can't battle the spirit of Diabolis, but you are virtually the equivalent to a spirit, so . . ."

Adrian now understood, but repeated back what he had heard. "So, when you say that things are made up of cheaper materials and they suddenly become more advanced. What you mean to say is that Diabolis is now a spirit and is more powerful than ever! And you want me, a simple aura, to battle him?"

"Correct!" the King said as a giant smile crept across his face. "Rhesus can't do it. Myself and all of my armies can't do it. But a solidified aura can!"

Adrian panicked. Butterflies in his stomach was an understatement. "I don't know. Are you sure it will work?"

"Positive!" the King responded. "Remember, the flag always flies proudest during the storm!"

Adrian nodded in agreement.

The King continued. "I know that at several times during this adventure you have probably thought very evil thoughts, and at other times you have thought very righteous thoughts. Your mind has contemplated both sides and sometimes you wonder what side you are on. But it is your actions that cast the deciding vote. You, Adrian, have proven yourself to be a righteous man."

"What if my anger slips out?"

"Then you must use it strictly against those who **transgress** against others . . . with no benefit to yourself of course. That is **what it means** to control your temper!" The King then reached under the **table and** pulled forth a large white box. Within the box was a Rike Air **Palmer, the** kind of gun Adrian had once used before to battle Diabolis. It was securely held in a black leather holster that also contained a long black whip. In another pocket was a small blue box, about the size of a ring box.

"What is that for?" Adrian asked.

"You will see," King Adam advised. "It is now time to go."

"What about my friends?"

"I will inform them of your great valor."

"At least I have Braddock!"

"Communication with Braddock will be temporarily cut off."

"What? I can't do it without Braddock!"

"You will do fine! You are half of Braddock anyway. You will know what to do."

Now Adrian was really scared. "Okay," he said uncertainly. He stood and secured the black holster around his waist. "I will trust you."

King Adam stood as well. "Good! Now, close your eyes, and I want you to picture the large green fingerprint!"

"How did you know about that?" Adrian asked. But before he could receive an answer there was a blinding flash of white light that forced his eyes shut. Shortly thereafter everything was pitch black and motionless. He dared not open his eyes, he just concentrated on the large green fingerprint. Another flash of white light followed and all was still. There was no sound. He suddenly felt a gentle breeze. Things were getting stranger by the minute.

Adrian slowly opened his eyes and much to his surprise found himself back on the planet Rolin, the four hundred mile inside-out planet where he had met Rhesus and Seth. He stood in the middle of the wheat field and had to pinch himself to make sure that he wasn't dreaming. He was very much awake and still very fearful of what was about to happen.

Fifty feet away the grass stirred. Something black rapidly slithered away. Adrian quickly drew his gun but the creature had vanished.

"I hope that was just a reozzy!" Adrian said to himself. He would much rather deal with a reozzy than the ghost of Diabolis right about now.

Everything remained quiet.

"Where are you!" Adrian called out, holding his gun more securely. "Come out you coward!"

The wind picked up and echoed a ghostly voice. "Coward?" it spoke. Diabolis suddenly appeared and plunged out of the wheat field wearing a pitch-black cloak and towered over Adrian in a giant plume of black smoke. "I am no coward!" he thundred.

Adrian couldn't speak. He fired his gun and a purple blast of compressed air belted from his gun and ripped through the black smoke.

Diabolis squealed in pain then regained his composer. "You can not kill me! I am a God!"

Adrian laughed. "You are a spirit! I am an aura! If I can die, you can die!"

"I CAN NOT DIE!"

Adrian aimed his gun at Diabolis again. "We'll see about that!"

Diabolis wrapped himself around Adrian like a python around its prey.

Adrian fired off three more shots of yellow, blue and red. All missed. He held his breath and stood his ground until Diabolis released his deadly grip and slithered away among the golden wheat like a snake.

Adrian ran after the creepy black shadow, now unafraid. He fired more rounds of green, orange and pink, but Diabolis was too slippery, he avoided each blast with quick turns and rolls.

Diabolis briefly disappeared and hit Adrian from behind.

Adrian knocked the madman back with two blasts of silver and gold.

The gold blast sheared Diabolis's right shoulder and once again allowed him to slither back into the grasses.

Diabolis led Adrian on a wild chase through the wheat for forty five minutes, while Adrian kept firing and releasing brown, yellow and white blasts. A tan bolt injured Diabolis's left leg, proving that even as a spirit Diabolis was weak. He only had the illusion of twisting his body into every shape and size to make himself appear bigger and stronger. But Adrian knew the truth; he had been worried for nothing.

The chase through the wheat raged on! The two men ran, slid and pounced on each other. The wheat was wearing away at Adrian's legs and began to slow him down. He pictured the green fingerprint in his mind's eyes and flew through the wheat like a super hero and landed on Diabolis's cloak. Diabolis cursed and soared high into the air. Adrian kept the fingerprint in his mind and held on tighter to Diabolis until the two men flew past the comet that had been the planet's sun, and were out in deep space.

The two enemies flew through space at the speed of light. Diabolis began kicking and tearing at Adrian's clothes and hair in an attempt the knock him loose.

Adrian held on tighter.

Diabolis had the upper hand; he was not half mortal like Adrian was, and so was far more flexible and agile. But still Adrian held on for dear life, until he noticed that they were sailing toward the planet, Deltena—the maroon and blueish planet that Adrian had once visited and walked through the frozen fog.

They landed harshly on the surface and were sent rolling by the force of their speed. Diabolis once again returned to his feet and floated away behind the soft purple, pink and pastel green rocks that made up the landscape.

Adrian was getting tired of this game of cat and mouse. He blasted one shot at every shadow in the mountainous area until he noticed one shadow that was on the wrong side of a small purple hill, it was facing the sun. How unusual? He blasted a yellow bolt of air and heard the shadow scream. Adrian quickly pounced and grabbed Diabolis around the neck, placing him in a headlock as soon as the despicable creature had reassembled himself back into a personage.

Diabolis squirmed fiercely and tried to sink his teeth into Adrian's arm, but Adrian just pictured the green fingerprint and watched as Diabolis's fangs passed right on through.

Adrian looked around the landscape and noticed the frozen fog. He didn't know if this was the same place that he, Rhesus and Seth and landed before, or if it was just another patch of fog that the planet probably had all over, but he didn't have time to analyze it. He dragged Diabolis over the loose pinkish soil and threw him in. Minutes passed and Adrian braved the cold briefly and went in to get him. Diabolis was frozen and was stiff as a board.

Adrian threw him to the ground and aimed his gun. This time it *was* over.

Diabolis smiled; the ice cracking at the movement of his sinister lips. He floated out of his frozen entrapment, leaving the ice that was now in the form of his personal image below. The ice crumbled into a million pieces as soon as Diabolis snapped his fingers.

Adrian gasped as Diabolis slowly grew five times his own size, then ten times, twenty times, forty times his own size until he filled the entire sky with his presence, blocking out the sun and making it appear as if it were the middle of the night. Adrian tried to fire six rounds of gold, blue, red, black, orange and maroon blasts, but nothing could faze the dark lord.

Adrian was snatched painfully from the ground and whisked up into the darkness of Diabolis's arms and once again out into the deepest reaches of space. Within an hour he found himself standing among the burnt rubble that used to be the majestic planet of Albeta. Gone were the buildings. Gone was the raging battle that had once made it look like an electric sun. Gone was the red, blue and green Wy-ok lazar beam missiles that had once orbited the planet. He was now in Diabolis's lair!

Diabolis quickly knocked the Rike Air Palmer from Adrian's hand and sent it tumbling into the darkness.

"No!" Adrian cried. He now felt completely helpless. He rapidly looked around for it, but it had vanished. Without thinking he grabbed his whip from his belt and lashed out at Diabolis.

Diabolis retaliated by pulling out a fire whip of his own. The whip glowed red-hot with the rage of a wild fire and illuminated the surrounding area with a reddish hue.

Adrian was suddenly scared again. He continued to crack his whip in the air but his small weapon was no match for Diabolis. He continued to try by waving his whip in the air above his head and bringing it down with a loud snap, but each time Diabolis would stop each blow in the middle of the strike by snagging it with his own flaming cord.

Adrian cracked his whip again just inches from Diabolis's head, then ran to a plume of smoke that was still billowing from some war-torn debris. He pictured the green fingerprint and began to climb up the smoke on his hands and knees.

Diabolis was right on his tail and closing in.

Adrian climbed faster until he reached the gray clouds that filled the sky and began to walk upright. The sensation of walking on clouds was something Adrian had never experienced before.

Diabolis floated above the clouds and closed in. He swept his whip at Adrian's feet—but Adrian jumped in the nick of time and returned to the soft cloud with a slight bounce.

Adrian advanced with four mighty blows, but Diabolis warded them off with one spin and two greater blows. Adrian tried the tactic again and succeeded in striking Diabolis in the torso. The evil master was briefly split in half and quickly reassembled himself. Adrian would not be so lucky if that kind of injury were to happen to him, and he knew it! If only he had a shield.

Diabolis was growing angrier. He tore at Adrian with more and more powerful blows. Adrian could only use his whip for defense.

Everything appeared in slow motion, and at other times it was too fast. The dueling man-form apparitions spiraled, jumped and ducked as the whips themselves screamed and cracked, while viciously slicing through the thick air.

Adrian managed to wrap his whip around Diabolis's left leg but couldn't pull it free. He forgot about the green fingerprint and fell through the cloud, landing on the ground and eventually rolled to a stop.

Diabolis shook Adrian's whip off his leg and followed, coming to land ten feet away from Adrian. "You are doomed!" he echoed with the roar of a thousand lions.

Adrian ran for shelter.

Diabolis's whip tore across Adrian's back.

Adrian screamed in pain. His clothes had protected him from most of the blow but he could still feel the sting. The intense heat from the whip could be felt all over his body from head to toe.

Diabolis was growing stronger.

Adrian reached the shelter of a burned, upside-down fighter craft and dove under the cockpit. He noticed that his clothes were on fire and quickly did a stop-drop-and-roll until the flames were extinguished. His heart was beating against his chest. He took a minute to briefly look around the cockpit at all of the burned control and navigational tools. Then turned his attention back to Diabolis.

Diabolis was drawing closer. He leaped up onto the fighter craft and began jumping up and down, crushing Adrian underneath.

Adrian felt his chest give way. He struggled for breath and tried to picture the green fingerprint, but it was no use, he fell unconscious. *He was dead.*

All was dark and silent. No noise could be heard . . . until, in the distance; the sound of chirping birds. Adrian slowly opened his eyes to find himself in heaven. He laid quietly among soft, green grass and stared up at beautiful, colorful flowers that grew along the walls of unique gray rock formations. The sky was bright blue with only a few puffy white clouds. He had lost the battle but it didn't seem to matter, he just laid there and peacefully absorbed the stimulating heat from the golden sun. It felt so much better than the cold, damp, darkness that he had felt before.

Suddenly there was another noise that seemed completely out of place. It was coming from about fifty feet above Adrian's head. Adrian rolled over with a smile that quickly faded as soon as he saw the origin of the noise.

Diabolis was digging his grave. He had not died at all! He was on the garden planet of Galla.

Diabolis was standing knee deep in a six foot long hole, and was digging deeper with a black spade.

Adrian jumped to his feet, almost tripping, and charged at the evil being. He had no weapon so he would have to use his bare hands.

Diabolis turned around and was very surprised to see that his victim was still alive. "Stop!" he ordered.

Adrian stopped but shouldn't have.

Diabolis stepped out of the grave and threw the black spade to the ground. "I'm glad to see you here," he scoffed.

Adrian knew he was lying.

"Now you can witness my greatest transformation!" Diabolis laughed. "In life I was powerless, but in death I am all powerful!"

Adrian tightened both of his fists. He could feel beads of sweat trickling down his forehead. "What do you plan to do?" he asked, controlling his temper.

"I will turn myself into a planet! A great and powerful orb! I will destroy all! My revenge will be great and swift! And you can not stop me!"

Adrian was thrown to the ground by a great, unseen force, as Diabolis began to spin faster than he had ever done before. The wind blew like a dark tornado and raged on like a powerful hurricane. It was too much for Adrian to endure, but he had to try. He staggered to his feet and just about reached Diabolis when the wind suddenly stopped. After the black smoke had departed and was slowly carried away by the gentle breeze, Adrian beheld the new planet. It was an exact replica of our planet Mars—but was the size of Adrian's fingernail.

Adrian couldn't help but laugh as all fear left his body. "Well," he said, "I guess all things are relative!"

All at once the planet began to depart. Adrian ran toward it and extended his arm, but the tiny red planet was just out of reach from his fingers and soared high into the sky.

"No!" Adrian cried. He had to get that planet! He couldn't be so close and let it slip through his fingers again. But How? The tiny orb was flying too fast for him to climb a tree or anything else. What could he do? He had to think fast!

"Throw me!" A voice said.

Adrian looked around. "What?" he said.

"Throw me!" The voice said again.

"What?" Adrian repeated.

Suddenly Cree-L jumped out of Adrian's pocket. "Throw me, you idiot!"

Adrian was surprised. He had completely forgotten that Cree-L was with him.

"Throw me! Now!"

"I can't throw you! You would get hurt," Adrian said.

"It won't hurt as bad as some of the things that I've already been through! Now throw me!"

Adrian snatched the little from the ground, took aim, and threw him as hard as he could.

Cree-L flew through the air head first, quickly grabbed the fleeing planet in mid air with both hands, and came to land softly in some soft green foliage.

Adrian ran to his aid and found him unharmed and sitting on a large green leaf. The planet was trying to free itself by shaking the little man as hard as he could, but Cree-L was holding it down with the weight of his little body. Adrian grabbed Cree-L with his left hand and grasped the tiny planet with his right thumb and index finger.

"We did it! We won!" Cree-L cheered, as Adrian returned him to his shirt pocket.

"Yes we did!" Adrian said, eyeing the small insignificant replica of Mars. Then he remembered the small blue box that King Adam had given to him. He opened it with one hand and looked inside. Within, was a small red pill capsule. He handed the pill to Cree-L to have him open it, and when this task was done, Adrian shoved the red planet inside and resealed the pill.

The pill began to shake violently. Adrian thought nothing of it and slipped the pill into the blue box. "Let's go home," he said.

"What will happen to the planet?" Cree-L asked.

"King Adam will destroy it."

"Is there life on that planet?"

"I don't think so, but you never know."

20

Stasia

168 hours later, on the frozen planet of Seeknom . . .

Adrian ran his hand over the smooth, frozen ice, probing for the slightest crevice in which to place his hand and pull himself up. He swung his pick high above his head and brought it smashing into the frozen cascade, sending large chunks of ice tumbling down over his body.

High above on the ice summit, Doblin held the rope securely and watched his two friends Adrian and Suca dangle dangerously below, attached to the mountain by only their heavy spike-boots. "A little farther!" he called. He reached his large hand down and pulled the two exhausted men up and onto the peak. "Good work," he encouraged.

Adrian smiled, took hold of the grip on the zip-line, and leapt off the edge of the peak on the other side. He flew through the air, racing down the cord, and enjoyed the quick rush, until he came to land in a gust of powdery white snow.

Somewhere amid the white sky that met the white snow, Stasia's beautiful voice filled the air. "You could have killed yourself!" she yelled, rushing to Adrian's side.

"No, it was a blast," Adrian said, dusting the snow off his thick fur coat.

Stasia giggled threw her arms around Adrian's neck, and kissed his stiff frozen lips. "Let's go back inside," she said, rubbing his chin with her delicate finger.

Adrian turned and looked at the two small figures of Doblin and Suca that remained far away at the top of the ice ridge. He waved briskly several times and watched his friends do the same. There had never been a happier time in his life. He placed his arm around Stasia's shoulders and together the two of them made their way back to King Adam's new ice palace.

Once inside Adrian filled his lungs with the smell of the brand new building. "Great to be alive, isn't it?!"

"That it is!" a voice said from behind, over the sound of a small electric motor.

Adrian turned to see his old friend Seth Biggs approach, riding an upright, two-wheel, electronic wheelchair. He rode up and stopped at eye level.

"How do you like my gadget?" Seth said. "It's based on balance, but at times I'm not so sure about that."

"It's great!" Adrian answered. "What did the doctors say?"

"Diabolis just stunned my muscular system, but I should be as good as new in a couple of months."

"A couple of months, wow!" Adrian responded.

"Oh, that's nothing," Seth said, spinning his chair, "as long as I get to keep my new toy."

At that time, Rhesus entered out of the chamber where he had been in conference with the King. "Hey, Adrian, are you and Stasia going to go to the celebration we are having on the Covey moons?"

"Yeah, definitely! We wouldn't miss it for the worlds!"

"Hey, I got an idea," Stasia interrupted. "Why don't we go for a walk down on the beach."

"Sounds good," Adrian said. Then he turned back to Rhesus. "Life doesn't get any better than this, eh?" he said, patting Rhesus on his shoulder, then he walked off.

Seth looked at Rhesus with an expression of hopelessness. "Yeah, that Stasia only likes Adrian for his brain; it's the small things in life that count."

"I heard that!" Adrian called back.

Seth quickly pulled his had down over his eyes.

"Come on, Biggs, let's get out of here."

Stasia and Adrian quietly walked hand in hand to the indoor beach. They stood barefoot on the rocks, listening to the slow waves calmly lapping against the shore while sea-gulls squawked and circled high above in the exquisite white dome ceiling.

Stasia's beautiful hair blew gently in the warm wind. "Come on," she said, running down off the rocks and to the water.

Adrian followed, passing through a couple trees, when Braddock's image suddenly appeared, catching him off guard. Adrian ducked to miss the upcoming branches, but they sliced along his right cheek.

"Hello!" Braddock said. "We've got some unbelievable news! I'm so excited! Devon and I have been poring over ideas and plans, and we think we've come up with a way to bring you back."

"That's great," Adrian said, rubbing his scratched face.

"You seem less than thrilled. Is there something wrong?"

"Oh, no, you just caught me off guard, that's all."

"I'm sorry, we'll have to work on that. Maybe I can add more power to the channel and activate and audio signal of some sort."

"That sounds like a plan."

"Anyway," Braddock continued, "we've developed the basis for a very intricate plan. We will lift you out of your microscopic worlds by temporarily scrambling the materials that make you up and bring you back to the surface in a specially designed teleporter. Once you arrive back here, the release of pressure on your body will dilute and you should return to your natural size again."

"Can Stasia come?"

"Who is Stasia?"

"Oh, the most wonderful girl in the world! She is King Adam's daughter," Adrian said, then went on to tell Braddock of Diabolis's defeat.

"Hmmm, I don't think it's possible to bring Stasia back with you. The human body would be very, very difficult to reassemble after traveling through a teleporter, If it can be done at all! I'll tell you what, I'll work on it!"

"I hope it can work, I'd love for you to meet her."

"Yes. It will be some time, though; the plan we've worked out will probably take up to a year or more. My guess is more."

"That's all right, I've already made plans with Cree-L to return to Galla and help build his city, not to mention rebuilding the millions of other planets.

Braddock paused. "So, we're probably looking at bringing you back in five millennium."

"No, go ahead and build your teleporter, maybe I can commute back and forth."

"You sure are making things difficult for me."

Adrian laughed. "We'll work something out."

"Yes, we will," Braddock said. "It always works out. But for now I need to talk to Devon. We'll see you later."

"Bye!" Adrian said, as Braddock's transmission cut out. He smiled contentedly and watched Stasia run along the water's edge.

Adrian never knew how this adventure began. He never knew birth, and as far as he was concerned, he never existed before he met Braddock. But now he wondered if there had been a life long ago that he had forgotten. Someday, perhaps, he would find the answer. It was as much of a mystery as the destiny that awaited him in the future—and he was loving every minute of it!

* * *

It is rumored that Cree-L returned to Marrek's Mercantile, stepped into the fruit growing machine, and grew, and grew, and grew. But that's another story.

*Do you have any short stories about Adventures With Boys that you would like to share? E-mail them to grantlee3000@hotmail.com.

*Also by G.L. Strytler:
Adventures With Boys #1 The Great Time-Link Photography Project.
Adventures With Boys #2 Instru-Mental.